NEVER TOO OLD

by

Mary Oertel-Kirschner

Mary Oertel-Kirschner

www.abqpress.com

www.abqpress.com
Albuquerque, New Mexico

ISBN 978-1-63587-222-4

For all of my "older" friends,
who still feel the same on the inside,
though their outside may have changed a bit.

CHAPTER ONE

Blanche Harriman was making an entrance. She tossed her emerald scarf over the shoulder of her fuchsia jumpsuit—a riveting combination for a redhead—while her eyes swept the sun-filled breakfast room to catch sight of Margaret. It was past eight-thirty. She thought she was the one who'd be late, but she'd lucked out. Margaret wasn't here yet.

"Good morning," she called gaily to Ruby Goldmark and Esther Zamora, two friends who were sipping coffee and reading the morning paper at a table next to the juice bar. She waved to half a dozen others as she swished past their tables heading for a place near the window.

The "breakfast room" was a section of the elegant dining room at La Mesa del Sol, a posh retirement compound perched amid manicured lawns and flower beds about a mile north of the Santa Fe Plaza. Blanche liked sitting near a window where she could look out over the city with its stunning backdrop of the Sangre de Cristo Mountains, aptly named for the blood-red color they took on at sunset.

"I'll have the mix, please," Blanche told the breakfast hostess who appeared with two steaming pots of coffee, regular and decaf. Having half of each was her recipe for caffeine control. "But I'll wait for Miss Forbes before ordering."

Sunlight streaming in through the window highlighted the lively color of Blanche's hair, a tumble of reddish waves that looked, to the uninformed, as though they hadn't spent much time with a hairbrush. It actually had taken twenty minutes of concentrated effort to achieve the *au courant* look that Lauren, her stylist, recommended. She checked her watch again. Unusual for Margaret to be late.

"Been stood up?"

Frank Zanders was passing by her table with a copy of *The New York Times* tucked under his arm. His eyes twinkled behind his thick lenses and he was wearing one of his trademark bow-ties, navy with yellow polka dots.

"Margaret's running late this morning," she said. "She was supposed to meet me at eight-thirty."

He winked. "Maybe she's sleeping in. Might have had a late night out on the town."

Blanche twirled a henna curl around her index finger and watched Frank, in his expanse of seersucker, amble on through the dining room. He *definitely* was flirting with her. Last week, when she'd been wearing her gold caftan by the pool, he'd told her she looked like an exotic butterfly.

As it happened, she did know what time Margaret had come in last night. She'd been out on the patio around nine, applying a final coat of rouge royal on her nails and watching the moon edge up over the mountains. The magic of the moment had been marred by Jack Forbes, Marga-

ret's nephew, roaring up in his red sports car to deposit her at the front entrance. He tore off crazily, spewing gravel on the drive. Blanche was so startled she got a glob of polish on her little finger.

Now it was almost nine in the morning. Blanche decided to go ahead and order the raspberry crepes when her waitress stopped by her table for the third time. In fact, she put in a double order, knowing Margaret loved raspberries. Certainly she'd be along any minute.

Darn, she chastised herself. She should have brought that irksome cell phone that her daughter, Mitzi, insisted she carry. Then she could have given Margaret a buzz.

I'm sure I got it right, she mused. Margaret was so specific about wanting to meet this morning—early, she'd said. She said they needed to fortify themselves with breakfast.

It had sounded quite intriguing. Margaret said something was eating at her, that she thought something strange was going on at La Mesa. She wouldn't say what it was. She needed to check on something first. Then she wanted to chew it over with Blanche.

Blanche didn't like to be left dangling, but Margaret held firm. "Just hold your horses 'til Monday," she said. "Then get ready to put that razor-sharp brain of yours to work."

"You lose a lot of brain cells by seventy-eight," Blanche had reminded her.

"Not you," Margaret had returned. "You're still growing them like bugs in a petri dish."

* * *

Blanche had known Margaret Forbes for nearly fifty years, from the time they met as young school teachers back in Birch, Minnesota. They hit if off that first year and remained close through all the twists and turns their lives subsequently took. Blanche married a handsome insurance salesman, Arthur, and they eventually produced a baby girl, Mitzi. At that point, Blanche turned in her chalk for diaper pins. Meanwhile, Margaret went on climbing her career ladder and over the years spread more and more territory between herself and Birch. First it was St. Louis for graduate school, then Denver, and ultimately Santa Fe where she settled in as superintendent of schools.

Margaret was among the first to be called when Blanche's comfortable world was ripped apart three years ago. Arthur suffered a sudden, fatal heart attack just like that, while driving home on an ordinary Tuesday afternoon. The weeks and months after his death were wrenching for Blanche, but it never occurred to her to leave Birch.

The idea of going to Santa Fe popped out of the blue right before the holidays just a year ago, the second Christmas without Arthur. Mitzi and Ed and the kids were making plans to visit Ed's parents in Ohio. They wanted Blanche to come too, same as last year. "We'll all be together again," Mitzi urged.

One of Blanche's most vivid memories of that Christmas was how Ed's folks kept their T.V. blasting throughout dinner. When they talked, it was only to criticize—Democrats, Republicans, Greens, Independents, Catholics, Jews,

Episcopalians, Baptists, anybody that breathed, it seemed. And there was no escape because it was ten below zero outside with six feet of snow on the ground. She found it difficult to be frank with Mitzi for fear of irrevocably wounding her. Still, she knew she couldn't bear to go through that scene again, so in a sudden, panic-driven inspiration, she devised a brilliant lie. She told Mitzi she'd already made plans to spend Christmas with Margaret Forbes in Santa Fe.

"What a great idea!" Margaret said when Blanche called to invite herself. "Why not pack up and move here permanently? It's the lap of luxury. The biggest decision you'll ever have to make is what to order for breakfast."

It was luxurious all right, and worth all the arguments she'd had to muster for Mitzi when she put her house on the market in Birch. She plucked the last raspberry from her plate and dabbed her lips with a pale pink linen napkin. And now if Margaret's arthritis didn't flare up, they'd be going to Cozumel this Christmas. That would take care of Ohio, and the even stickier possibility that the whole troop might come to Santa Fe.

By quarter of ten Blanche took her final sip of coffee. The staff was clearing tables, and the order of crepes for Margaret was limp and cold on the plate. Could she just have forgotten? Not like her at all. Blanche set down her napkin and decided to go upstairs and see what happened.

She had just slid her chair back from the table and was rising when she saw Christine Wilson, the attractive director of La Mesa's nursing services, come in. Christine was scanning the dining room, obviously looking for someone. She locked her eyes on Blanche and walked briskly over to her.

"Mrs. Harriman, I was hoping I'd find you here. I knocked on your door, but didn't get an answer. I thought you might still be at breakfast." She put a hand gently on Blanche's arm. "Please, sit down."

Blanche sat back down, puzzled by Christine's manner.

"It's Margaret. I'm terribly sorry, I know you were very close."

"What's the matter? Where is she?" Blanche felt her chest tighten.

Christine's usually smooth forehead was furrowed with concern and her blue eyes searched Blanche's as though to measure the effect of what she was about to say. "I'm so sorry."

"She was supposed to meet me here more than an hour ago."

"I'm afraid she won't be coming," Christine said. "Last night. . ." she hesitated. . . "I got a call from Vangie around midnight last night. . ."

Vangie, one of the registered nurses on the staff who helped residents with chronic problems and attended minor emergencies, was on duty Sunday nights.

"What happened?" Blanche's stomach began doing flip-flops with the crepes.

"The hall monitor noticed Margaret's beads weren't outside around eleven o'clock. She reported it to the nurses' station and Vangie tried calling. When she didn't get an answer, she went to her apartment. She found Miss Forbes on the bedroom floor."

The bead system was simple. Residents were asked to put a string of red wooden beads on their outside doorknobs each evening when they retired, as a sign that all

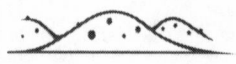

was well. In the morning they would remove them to indicate they were up and functioning as usual. Blanche had caused several false alarms before she devised a foolproof reminder for herself: she kept her beads wrapped around the handle of her toothbrush.

"Is she all right?" Blanche's voice was rising.

"I'm afraid not," Christine said gently. She reached across the table for Blanche's hand.

Blanche stared at her, hearing her words, but struggling against them as though they were coming through a heavy fog.

"Dr. Hillman came right away, but he couldn't revive her," Christine said. "It was too late."

"Too late?" Blanche's green eyes, so carefully accented with mascara, widened in horror.

"I'm sorry," Christine said very softly. "She had a heart attack."

"But. . .we were supposed to meet here for breakfast this morning," Blanche repeated lamely.

"I know, I know," Christine said soothingly, still holding her hand. "I'm so sorry."

"She's. . . dead?" This couldn't be happening.

Christine nodded as she gently squeezed Blanche's hand. "We've been trying to call her nephew, but we haven't been able to reach him yet. Is he the only relative?"

"Yes, Blanche said. "Jack is the only one."

* * *

Blanche knew they were doing their best to wrap themselves protectively around her. Juanita Gomez, the homemaker's helper she shared with Margaret for a few hours

each week, guided her into a chair. Christine Wilson handed her a pill and told her to take it.

Blanche looked at the two women, going from Christine's China blue eyes to Juanita's black ones, and thought they were just strangers, kindly strangers who were trying to help. What she really wanted now was to be alone, to try and take in the enormity of what had happened by absorbing one little edge at a time. Staunch, crusty, indomitable Margaret—how could she be gone?

"I'll leave you to rest for a while," Christine said, seeming to read her thoughts. "Juanita will let me know if you need anything."

Margaret had recommended Juanita Gomez to Blanche when she moved in. She was employed by the housekeeping department but earned extra money on the side by helping a few residents with small tasks—ironing, cleaning, sometimes running an errand. She'd come to the U.S. from Mexico with a work permit about a year ago and spoke mostly Spanish, though Blanche suspected she understood more English than she let on.

Now Blanche watched as Juanita silently went about heating water in the small kitchen which opened to the living room. She was preparing a steaming cup of chamomile tea for her.

"She has *familia*? Juanita asked, mixing Spanish and English.

"*Solo* her *sobrino*, only her nephew, Jack," Blanche answered in simple Spanish. "You've met him, no?"

"*Sí.*" Juanita handed her the mug of tea. "*Yo lo recuerdo.*" I remember him.

"She never married, and her brother died years ago," Blanche continued. "Jack is the only one left." She heard

her own words as though she were talking from far away, a faint voice in the corner of a big room. She had a fleeting thought that there'd been some mistake and that Margaret would come rushing in any minute now, apologizing for missing breakfast. In her mind, she replayed what Christine had told her, trying, absurdly, to see if there was something she'd misunderstood. It all seemed surreal.

* * *

Blanche was floating in disconnected thoughts, numbed by the effects of the pill Christine Wilson had administered before leaving. A sudden loud knocking at the front door jarred her back to reality. Juanita went to answer it.

"Mrs. Harriman, I've just heard the distressing news." Reverend Kenneth Adams, in a white Western-style shirt with a turquoise and silver bolo tie in the shape of a cross, stood in the doorway looking past Juanita as if she weren't there.

"May I come in?" He stepped smoothly in without waiting for a response and went to Blanche who hadn't moved from the overstuffed reading chair Juanita had ushered her into an hour ago. He reached for her hand, and after an awkward hesitation, she gave it to him.

"The Lord giveth and the Lord taketh away," he said, looking earnestly into her eyes. "I pray her soul will rest in peace."

It was bizarre that Adams, of all people, should be trying to comfort her for Margaret's death, Blanche thought. Margaret could barely stand the self-appointed evangelist who ingratiated himself with the wealthy widows at La

Mesa. She had hated his holier-than-thou posturing on ethical issues and she'd doubted his sincerity. Nonetheless, Blanche felt tears sting at her eyes and blinked hard to stop them. She didn't want to break down in front of Adams.

He leaned close, patting her hand.

"Time heals all wounds. The good Lord's infinite strength will see you through."

Blanche studied his narrow face, his thin lips, the soft brown eyes oozing concern. He had all the right gestures, but she wasn't buying it. His words sounded too perfect, as though they'd been rehearsed many times. Besides, what she'd heard about him from Margaret didn't endear her to him.

Adams was minister of a small congregation called "All God's Children", leaving him plenty of time to spend at La Mesa del Sol "collecting stray souls and stray bank accounts," Margaret loved to say. Blanche had a sudden uncharitable thought that he might be trying to manipulate her for a contribution, something in memory of Margaret. But at least the thought helped to bring her back under control, and she cleared her throat deliberately. "Perhaps the Reverend would like a cup of tea?" she said, turning to Juanita and slipping her hand out from Adams'.

"It's a blessing that she went quickly," he said.

"A blessing that she's dead?" Blanche raised her voice.

"Now, now, Mrs. Harriman. It was a blessing that she didn't have to suffer long."

"But there was nothing wrong with her. We were supposed to meet for breakfast."

"These things happen. They're out of our hands."

"She had some arthritis, that's all."

"Obviously her heart was not strong," Adams said patiently.

"Her heart was fine!" Blanche heard the testiness in her voice but didn't care.

"Just reporting what Dr. Hillman said." He raised his hands in mock defense. "He warned her to take things easy, but as we all know, that wasn't her style."

"I never heard about any problem with her heart," Blanche insisted.

"Perhaps she didn't want to worry you."

Blanche weighed the possibility of Margaret not confiding in her about a heart condition so as not to worry her. It was exactly what Arthur had done, kept his weakened heart a secret from her for years, and she'd only extracted the information out of the doctor after his death. She didn't believe Margaret would have deceived her, knowing how deeply hurtful Arthur's secret had been. In fact, she was sure of it.

But she didn't want to discuss it further with this cow-eyed minister who sat there staring at her. She sighed loudly and closed her eyes, sealing in tears of frustration and grief.

Juanita seemed to know what was needed.

"*Señora* Harriman must rest, *ahora,* now," she said firmly to Reverend Adams.

Adams looked confused for a second. But then he realized that he was being dismissed and set down his tea cup.

"Let me know if there is anything I can do."

Blanche nodded halfheartedly, her eyes still closed against the tears.

"I'll remember her in my prayers," he said.

Margaret would roll over in her grave if she could hear that, Blanche thought as the door closed behind him.

* * *

Juanita heated chicken soup for lunch, and Blanche poked at it distractedly.

"Miss Wilson, she said to make sure that you rest," Juanita said, plumping up the purple and turquoise throw pillows on Blanche's white couch. "Perhaps you would like to rest here?"

Blanche couldn't help smiling. Juanita may not say much, but she had a way of directing things.

"Thank you, Juanita."

Juanita put a note on the door which said "resting" so Blanche wouldn't be disturbed. She seemed hesitant about leaving, but Blanche knew that her regular housekeeping shift began at one o'clock. She reassured her she'd be all right.

Alone at last, Blanche allowed her anguish to overcome her. She knew now that it was real, that her closest friend for more than half her life was irrevocably gone. The held-back tears finally were released and they came in a great gush. Her shoulders heaved and her breath caught in little gasps and she wept as she hadn't since Arthur died. Finally the sobbing gave way to sheer fatigue and she closed her stinging eyes. She was drained.

She'd call Mitzi in a little while, she told herself. And Jack, she must reach him later with her condolences. First though, she would try to rest. She let her head sink into the soft pillows and took several deep, slow breaths. The image of Christine walking across the breakfast room to

tell her about Margaret kept flashing across her mind, but she worked to deflect it with a relaxation exercise she'd learned in yoga. There was an angel, a strong Italian angel, hovering over her with a huge watering can filled with white light, showering her with soothing sprays, sending warm, healing energy into every crevice of her body, down into her toes. The angel was telling her to rest, over and over, until eventually, gratefully, she managed to slide into a surface-skimming sort of sleep.

But around three-thirty, Blanche woke with a start. She felt as though something deep inside had jarred her.

She had one of those odd, disconnected flashes of memory. Once, when she was a little girl, she'd dropped her mother's favorite vase and cracked it. She turned it to the wall, hoping that her mother wouldn't notice. But of course she did. It was inevitable.

Something felt cracked now, and turned to the wall. She pulled back her hair from her forehead, damp with perspiration, and pictured Margaret as she'd last seen her. All that vitality, those alert eyes, her erect carriage. What was it she was so intent on telling her this morning?

Margaret had been mysterious about "something strange going on" at La Mesa. She was trying to figure something out. She had something else to do. . .something else to get. . . What could it have been about?

Blanche bolted upright, fully awake now, as she tried to recall Margaret's exact words. She said she had to *check on something first.*

Then she said she'd be needing Blanche's help, which meant it was something serious. She said to have her brain ready to go to work.

Blanche was concentrating so hard she was holding her breath.

Could it be. . .?

No, that was crazy.

She let out her breath in a rush, trying to push the thought from her mind.

Maybe it was true about Margaret's heart.

But she used to brag about her heart. Blanche could hear her saying, "It's so strong it'll keep on beating long after the rest of me is gone." They'd giggled like school girls over that.

The darker thought pressed itself forward. What if it wasn't a heart attack? What if Margaret had gotten involved in something dangerous? What it she'd learned about something she wasn't supposed to know? What if someone wanted to make sure she didn't do anything about it?

* * *

Blanche called Mitzi in Phoenix around suppertime. As a young girl, Mitzi had spent her school vacations at the Forbes' summer home on Lake Superior. She was a teenager before she realized that Margaret was not her real "auntie", not by blood anyway.

"Oh, Mom, I'm so sorry. How did it happen?"

"They say it was a heart attack."

"Did she have heart trouble?"

"No," Blanche said firmly, "At least I never heard about it, and I doubt very much that she would have kept that from me. She used to brag about her heart being strong. Her arthritis kicked up at times, but that was all."

"Maybe she didn't want to worry you if she had a heart condition."

"I can't believe she'd do that. She knew about your father. She'd never do that to me."

"A lot of people have heart attacks unexpectedly," Mitzi said, trying to be consoling. "It often happens that way, especially when you're over eighty."

Blanche didn't find the comment comforting. She weighed out whether to mention what Margaret had said about something "strange" going on at La Mesa, but decided Mitzi wouldn't give that any credence. She'd probably think Margaret was exaggerating.

"Mom?" Mitzi interrupted the momentary silence.

"What?"

"Are you all right?"

"I'll be OK. Just trying to take this in. It's hard."

"Maybe I ought to come over to Santa Fe."

"No, Mitzi, please." She didn't want to deal with Mitzi right now, not on top of everything else. "I'll be fine, really."

"Do you have some friends there?"

"Of course I have friends," she said, a slight edge in her voice. She'd met a lot of people at La Mesa, many through Margaret. She wasn't sure whether they were *truly friends*, except for Ruby and Esther, and maybe Frank Zanders. She hadn't known any of them all that long. Actually, she felt pretty alone at the moment, but she wasn't about to admit it to Mitzi.

"Mom, I know this is hard for you, but you're going to have to try and accept it," Mitzi said before hanging up. "I know you'll miss her, but these things happen and there's not much we can do about it."

Blanche had no response to that.

"Give me a call if you'd like to come over to Phoenix for a visit and I'll make the arrangements," Mitzi said. "It would be good for you to get away."

"I'm fine here. This is my home," Blanche said, trying to control her irritation.

What did Mitzi think anyway, that she couldn't take care of herself?

CHAPTER TWO

Blanche got out of bed and reached for her robe, suddenly missing the old pink chenille with the nap worn off at the elbows. She'd given it away when she moved to Santa Fe and bought a white kimono splashed with orange hibiscus blossoms in its place. The kimono seemed garish and foreign now, something left in her closet by an overnight guest.

Slipping into her fuzzy mules, she padded to the front door to retrieve the morning paper and take it into the small kitchen where her coffee maker was already sputtering. She wondered if there'd be an obituary notice this soon, and was startled to find a photo of Margaret staring at her from the front page.

"Ms. Forbes died around midnight Sunday of an apparent heart attack," the Capital News reported. Jack Forbes, Santa Fe stockbroker, was named as the only surviving relative. Margaret was praised for her years as superin-

tendent of the Santa Fe School District and for numerous other contributions to the community. The story tagged her an "heiress," referring to the family fortune built on iron mines in northern Minnesota.

Blanche remembered how Jack had been cut off from that fortune when he refused to stay up north and work for his father, Albert Forbes. He came to Santa Fe instead, and Margaret helped get him started as a stockbroker at Quenton and Co. She gave Quenton her fortune to invest, and they took on Jack as a trainee.

Jack had always struck Blanche as a lonely, rather sullen young man. She'd once commented to Margaret that it must be hard to go through life never having your father's approval.

Margaret said it was time he stopped pouting and grew up. "Born with a silver spoon in his mouth but never learned to feed himself," was the way she'd put it.

The newspaper fell to Blanche's lap as she thought about the way Margaret could sum up a situation with a one-liner like that. She pictured her as she'd last seen her, wearing her silver squash blossom necklace, with her thick silvery hair perfectly coiffed. Even at eighty-two, she was still an imposing figure, full of life, with a forceful personality. Some people were put off by her caustic comments, but that didn't make Margaret temper herself. "If you can't take the heat, stay out of the kitchen," she'd say.

Blanche checked the time. It was a little after eight. She'd tried calling Jack last night but hadn't gotten an answer. Maybe she could catch him now, before he left for work.

The telephone rang four or five times before a groggy voice said "H'llo."

"Jack? It's Blanche Harriman. I hope I haven't called too early."

Jack yawned audibly. "No, it's fine."

"I'm so sorry about Margaret," she said. "It's such a shock."

"Yeah, it happened fast. Heart attack."

"We were supposed to meet for breakfast, but she. . . she never came."

"Huh."

"She never said anything to me about having heart trouble. Did you know?"

"Not really," Jack said. "But then, she didn't exactly confide in me. The doc said she had some condition "

"I was waiting for her in the breakfast room," Blanche repeated as though her location when she learned of Margaret's death was somehow significant. "She said she wanted to talk to me about something."

"Yeah?"

"She said there was something strange going on over here at La Mesa. Did she say anything to you?"

"About what?"

Jack was either thick or deliberately being difficult.

"About something going on at La Mesa. She was trying to find out more about it."

"That's wild. No idea."

"When did you last see her?"

"Well, as a matter of fact, we had dinner Sunday night."

"Did she seem different to you or say anything unusual?" Blanche got a flash of herself as a special investigator trying to get the witness to reveal a critical piece of information.

"What is this, 'The Inquisition?'"

"I just thought something might have come up."

"Just the same old stuff. She was always on my case."

"Was she upset?"

"No more than usual."

"Enough to give her a heart attack?"

"Now, wait a minute," Jack said, his voice rising. "Are you suggesting I gave her a heart attack?"

"I'm just trying to find out what happened," Blanche said sweetly. She hesitated. "Have you thought about an autopsy?"

"Are you serious? What for?"

"It's possible she didn't die from a heart attack."

"What do you think she died from?"

"What if someone"—Blanche searched for the right words—"deliberately silenced her?"

"Deliberately silenced her? Come on, Mrs. Harriman. You've been watching too many movies."

"Well. . ." Blanche faltered.

"Look, my aunt was eighty-two years old. A lot of people have heart attacks by that age."

Blanche bit her lip.

"I know you two were friends for a long time, but the fact is, she got overly excited about stuff," he said. "Like this 'strange stuff' she was going to tell you. Who knows what that was all about."

"It could have been something very important," Blanche said.

He heaved a loud sigh. "Look," he said, changing the subject, "I've arranged for a memorial service at La Mesa. You'll be getting a notice today."

"Here?"

"Yeah, Reverend Adams will do it in the auditorium."

"Adams? Margaret couldn't stand him!"

"Is that right?" Now Jack's voice was patronizing.

"They could hardly say a civil word to each other."

"He called and said he'd like to do her memorial service."

"Your aunt would be furious if she knew," Blanche said.

"Well, that's not something we have to worry about, is it?" he said.

* * *

Jack hung up the telephone and stared into space for a few minutes. "That old bitch, what was she up to this time?" he said aloud. His head was starting to throb. He massaged his temples and grunted himself out of bed and into the bathroom. The past forty-eight hours had been unreal. On Sunday night, Margaret springs the news that she's pulling out her entire account from Quenton and Company. His reaction? He goes out and gets drunk with Alan Forrester, another broker. Dumb, very dumb.

Then on Monday, Margaret turns up dead.

Jack staggered towards the kitchen. He found a sticky jar of instant coffee and dropped a large spoonful of freeze-dried granules into a mug of water and stuck it in the microwave. A minute later, coffee in hand, he wandered into the living room and slumped into a leather easy chair.

He never should have told Alan, he thought as he took a swallow of the bitter black liquid.

Alan had been a friend from the University of New Mexico who now worked at Quenton too. If he hadn't told him, no one would know.

Shit, why hadn't he just gone home after dropping the bitch off on Sunday?

But instead he went over to La Fonda to have a drink. He got so smashed that he couldn't drive. Drive, hell, he could hardly walk. Ended up passing out on Alan's couch and woke up with a terrible hangover. He felt so lousy he couldn't face going to the office so he had Alan drive him back to La Fonda where he'd left his car. He went home instead of going into the office. That's where he was when he got word his aunt was dead.

"Damn!" Jack pounded his fist on the arm of the chair, causing the inky coffee to splash and slurp out over the chair and floor.

"Shit!"

He charged back to the kitchen and threw the rest of the coffee into the sink while grabbing a towel.

He remembered Alan pumping him about why Margaret was closing out her account. He thought he'd been careful how he answered. He told him she was upset because she'd lost a little money in the market. Maybe two-hundred grand was more than a little, but he figured he didn't have to get specific about it.

Alan had pressed him about how frequently he executed trades for her.

Hell, everyone traded a lot.

Of course, there was a fine line between trading often and trading excessively, churning a large account to make a nice commission every time you bought or sold a stock for a client. That type of account management could cost a broker his license.

Jack knew the fine line very well. He walked it daily in managing his aunt's account.

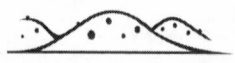

The old bat must have known it too, he realized now, but she'd said nothing for months. Then whammo, just like that, she announced she was done with him.

The bitch. She got what she deserved.

CHAPTER THREE

Christine Wilson sat behind her desk in the nursing office, her blue eyes puzzled. "Something strange going on at La Mesa? I can't imagine what she meant. Did she say anything else?"

"No, that's the problem," Blanche said. "She was trying to get a little more information before she could tell me about it. But I know it was something important."

Christine raised one eyebrow.

"You have to understand. Margaret rarely asked for help from anybody. She was a very self-sufficient type of person. But this time she actually said she was going to need my help."

"I see."

"Has anyone considered performing an autopsy?" Blanche wondered.

"An autopsy?" Both of Christine's eyebrows went up. "They only do an autopsy if there's some question about how the person died."

Blanche leaned forward and lowered her voice. "Has it occurred to you that this could all be connected?

"Connected?"

"She died just before she was going to tell me something important."

Christine's look hovered between tolerant and doubtful. She shifted in her chair.

"It's possible that her death wasn't totally natural you know," Blanche persisted.

"Wait, back up," Christine said. "She had a heart condition, not terribly serious, but significant considering her age. Maybe the timing was bad—it's never good—but the possibility of her having a heart attack is entirely plausible."

Blanche sat back, frowning. Everyone seemed to know about Margaret's heart except her. "I can't believe she wouldn't have told me if something was wrong. She used to brag about having a strong heart."

"I know this is hard," Christine said, her eyes soft with sympathy. "But probably the sooner you're able to accept it, the better it'll be."

Blanche, biting her lip, fought for control. "Is Vangie in?" she asked after a minute. "I'd like to talk with her."

"She ought to be done with her morning rounds," Christine said with a glance at her watch. "Let me buzz her."

Vangie Sanchez, RN, had been with La Mesa longer than most residents. Mid-forties, efficient, and good-humored, she was popular with everyone.

"I found her lying face down on the floor, just inside the bedroom," she told Blanche after she'd taken the other

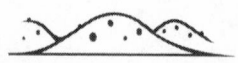

chair in Christine's office. "I knew right away it was bad. Her skin was mottled."

"Mottled?"

"Burst blood vessels," Vangie explained. "It often happens with a heart attack."

Blanche tried to picture Margaret's face as it must have looked.

"She went quickly," she added. "She was still warm when I tried CPR."

"What time was that?"

"Around eleven-thirty."

"And you called Dr. Hillman right away?"

Vangie nodded. "He was there in 15 minutes. But it was too late. She wasn't breathing, and there was no pulse."

"So there wasn't anything he could do?"

Vangie shook her head. "Nothing. She was gone."

* * *

Blanche sank into her bubble bath and reflected on what Christine Wilson had said. The sooner she accepted Margaret's death, the better it would be.

But that was the problem. She was having trouble accepting the whole thing, not just the fact that Margaret was dead, but the heart attack coming on so suddenly without warning. And she couldn't get the business of "something strange" out of her mind. It raised too many questions.

Blanche frowned in concentration, listening to the bubbles crack-popping around her.

Mitzi, Jack, Christine, Dr. Hillman—they weren't questioning the sudden death of an 82-year-old woman.

Having a heart attack at her age seemed a perfectly reasonable event.

Of course they hadn't been planning to go para-sailing
with her in Cozumel next winter. She was fit as a fiddle,
even if she was 82.

In her mind, Blanche went over and over what she
knew and what she didn't know until eventually the bubbles were gone and the water was starting to lose its comforting heat. It was time to get out. A plan that had been
slipping around the corners of her mind all morning was
getting clearer. As she ran a plump towel briskly over her
back, it came to final resolution. She splashed herself lib-
erally with Le Sin—a cologne sample she'd picked up at
Dillard's cosmetic counter. Then with a steady hand, she
applied jade green eye shadow, thick black mascara, and a
rosy blush over her sagging cheeks, the combination she
hoped would draw attention away from the dark puffiness
under her eyes. She needed to look good for this.

She flicked past dozens of dresses in the closet, briefly
considering a royal blue Dior suit from Ritzi Resale. Right
tone, but too warm. She returned to a chartreuse tunic
she'd bought for the Opera Guild reception. The sort of
dress that commanded attention, and she had the perfect
hat to go with it too, a big-brimmed straw with a lime green
band. She slipped the dress over her head and considered
her image in the bedroom mirror. Not bad, she decided.
Not bad at all.

She thought about calling J. J. Chavez, the front door-
man, to bring the Cadillac around for her but she didn't
want to get into a conversation about where she was going.
She'd just take the elevator down to the the parking garage
and get the car herself.

The gargantuan yellow Cadillac, a 1964 Fleetwood with vestigial fins—it was the last year for fins—had belonged to her late husband and Blanche kept it for sentimental reasons rather than practical ones. The thing was nearly twenty feet long, nearly impossible to park in Santa Fe, and it guzzled gas at an exorbitant rate. But she cherished the link with her past, with Arthur.

She thought of him now as she slid behind the wheel. If only he were here to help her think this through. He was so good on details; it was what had made him such a good claims adjustor, that and the fact that he always did his homework. Well, she'd try to do the same.

Of course, Arthur tended to be quite conservative. He might think it was a little premature for her to be going to the police.

She maneuvered the car through the electronically-controlled exit from the parking garage and drove slowly down the hill from La Mesa. It always took her a minute to get the feel of the big machine since she didn't drive it every day, sometimes not for weeks at a time, using La Mesa's van service instead. But she'd had the spring tune-up, a kind of ritual she always performed as Arthur had, and the car responded smoothly to her touch.

Blanche crossed St. Francis Drive and curved around Villa Linda Mall, heading downtown. San Francisco Street wasn't the most direct route, especially since it was jammed with tourist traffic, but Blanche always liked to have a look at the colorful plaza, the heart of the City Different. Under the portal of the Palace of Governors, Indians from nearby pueblos laid out their turquoise and silver jewelry and clay pottery while visitors crammed for closer looks. She

inched along behind gawking tourists and headed north towards Washington St.

In front of the pueblo-style police station she followed a sign directing visitors to park in designated spaces in the rear. But after steering the big Caddy down the narrow drive, she found all visitors' slots were filled. There appeared to be one space at the end of a row of police cars though, and she headed towards it. Halfway in, she braked when she saw the small sign, "Chief." But after a second of hesitation she pulled the rest of the way in. No one was going to arrest her, she rationalized, not at her age, not dressed like this.

Stepping out, she smoothed the bright tunic, adjusted her hat, and took a deep breath.

"I would like to speak to someone about a recent death," she announced to a uniformed officer sitting at the front desk.

The officer, male and looking fresh out of the academy, looked a bit hesitant.

"I have a friend who died on Sunday. There are some lingering questions surrounding her death, and I would like to speak to someone about it." She concentrated on sounding matter-of-fact.

"Has this death been reported?"

"Oh heavens yes. It's been in all the news. I'm just here to tell what's *not* in the news."

"Just a minute please."

Blanche watched the young officer dial a number on his intercom.

"There's a woman here," he said, appraising Blanche as he spoke. "She wants to talk to someone about a death, something not in the news."

He turned back to Blanche. "Lieutenant Otero will see you. He's inside, second office on the right."

Blanche walked through a set of double doors and stopped at the second office on the right. A uniformed officer with a with a brass name plate identifying him as "Enrique Otero," sat behind a desk.

"I'm Blanche Harriman."

"Lieutenant Otero," he said, rising about an inch off his chair and extending a hand.

She shook it, hoping he didn't notice the moisture which had collected on her palm.

"Have a seat." He waved to two leather-looking chairs in front of the desk. "What can I do for you, ma'am?" Otero was a big guy, husky. His skin was dark and his close-cropped curly black hair was flecked with grey.

"I have some information that I think may be important," Blanche began. (There was a split-second flash of herself crossing enemy lines to tell the Allies that she's broken the German code.) She told Otero about Margaret Forbes and about the meeting they were supposed to have on Monday morning.

"She died before she could tell me anything about it," she finished. "Of course her death was attributed to a heart attack, but I'm beginning to wonder."

Otero raised one eyebrow. He glanced at her hat.

She thought he suppressed a faint smile of amusement.

"I think whatever it was she wanted to talk to me about may have been put her in some kind of danger," she added crisply.

"Danger? What sort of danger?"

"Her life," Blanche said, relishing her boldness. "I think all of this may be connected."

Otero nodded but his face revealed nothing.

"You see," Blanche said, leaning forward, "she used the word *strange* and she wasn't a person who'd exaggerate. When she said she'd be needing my help, I knew it had to be something serious. She hardly ever needed help with anything."

"And you have no idea what it was about?"

Blanche shook her head. "She said she had to get a little more information before she could tell me."

Otero nodded again.

"I've talked to the director of nursing, and I've talked with her nephew. Neither has any idea what it could have been, and frankly, it occurs to me that maybe I shouldn't be talking about this to everybody. Margaret was keeping plenty quiet, and I have to trust she had her reasons."

"What would you like us to do?"

"Poke around a little, ask some questions. See what you can find out. Discretely of course."

"Who was her doctor?"

"Avery Hillman. He's the staff doctor at La Mesa."

He scribbled the name on a pad.

"How old was your friend, Mrs. Harriman?"

"Eighty-two."

"How old are you, ma'am, if I may ask?"

"Seventy-eight." She gave him a steady stare, challenging him to make something of it.

"You knew Mrs. Forbes for a long time?"

"Fifty years," she emphasized.

"Well, ma'am, I don't know what we can do for you. It's not much to go on."

"The point is, the timing was too coincidental," Blanche said, leaning forward again. "Besides, she was in excel-

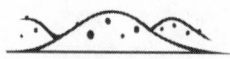

lent health. No heart trouble that I ever heard about, and believe me, I would have known. We told each other everything."

Lieutenant Otero raised his left eyebrow. "Do you know that for a fact?" he asked.

"Well, not absolutely," Blanche fumbled slightly. "They say she had some sort of heart condition, but I'm positive I would have known if it was anything significant."

"Mrs. Harriman, if there was anything unusual about her death, it would have been reported to us."

Blanche took a deep breath, her lips setting in a tight line.

"Look, ma'am, I'm really sorry about your friend," Otero said. "These things are hard to accept, especially when it's a good friend."

Blanche bit her lower lip.

"Look, I'll give Dr. Hillman a call. If there's any reason to take it further, I'll come round to La Mesa and talk to a few folks, all right?"

She nodded, having the feeling he merely was placating her and frustrated by the fact that she couldn't make him do more.

* * *

The dining room was buzzing. Blanche scanned the scene, hoping to spot Ruby Goldmark and Esther Zamora, two of Margaret's good friends who'd both slipped kind notes under her door. Not seeing them, she wound her way towards an empty table in the rear of the room.

"Mind if I join you?" Frank Zanders stood over her as she studied her menu. He wore a bow tie as usual, and a

light tan jacket which looked a bit tight across the front.

"Oh," Blanche said, surprised. "Please," she gestured for him to join her.

Zanders was the retired president of Santa Fe Mercantile Bank and she found him quite attractive though a bit on the portly side. When you get to my age, you can't be too picky, she'd thought often enough. And besides, he'd been close to Margaret.

"You're very dressed up this evening," he said, taking in the chartreuse tunic.

"I had to go to the. . .well, I had an errand in town."

"What looks good?" he asked cheerfully, scanning the menu.

"I'm having the salmon en croûte. Highly recommended by our waitress."

"I'm very sorry about Miss Forbes' death," Zanders said abruptly as though the words had been awaiting an opportunity to come out. "She spoke of you often and it seemed to give her such a lift when you moved here."

"A lift?" Funny, Blanche had never thought of Margaret needing a lift.

"Definitely."

"That's nice to hear."

"I used to manage her trust account when I was at the bank, and we got to be friends," Zanders said. "She still liked to talk with me about her portfolio, even though she'd moved everything over to Quenton."

"She must have valued your advice," Blanche said.

"She didn't get too much from that nephew of hers, I'm afraid."

"The boy with the silver spoon?"

He nodded. "They had their difficulties."

"I've heard some about it," Blanche said. Margaret had complained about Jack several times recently. She'd said they could hardly have a conversation without it erupting into an argument.

"She was thinking about going back to the bank," Frank said. Their waitress appeared to take their orders and ask if they'd like a glass of wine.

"You could probably use one," Frank encouraged. "A glass of chablis would go well with the salmon."

"Good idea," she said, wondering why she hadn't considered it herself.

"When I heard the news about Margaret, I came by your apartment," Zanders said when their waitress had left. "But I saw that sign on your door—that you were resting— so I didn't knock."

"You came by?"

"I know how close you were."

"That was thoughtful of you."

"Actually, I came by again this afternoon, but you weren't at home."

"You did?" Blanche felt a bit flustered. She could feel a blush start to warm her face. "I was at the police station," she said.

"Oh?" Zanders' eyes opened wider.

Blanche told him her story, taking pains to sound calm and rational. Arthur had always said one got further by presenting the facts calmly. She ended up by saying how sure she was that Margaret would have told her about a pre-existing heart condition.

"Interesting," Zanders said thoughtfully when she finished.

Finally, someone was taking her seriously.

"Any ideas what it was all about?" he asked.

"Zip," Blanche said, using an expression she had picked up from her granddaughter.

"She was no fool," he said, looking intently at her through his thick glasses.

"Exactly." This was more like it. (Another one of those instant flashes—the scene taking place in a little cafe in France. Frank would be in uniform, of course, and he would have a shock of unruly black hair tumbling down on his forehead.)

The waitress arrived with a small decanter of the house chablis. Frank poured them each a glass and then raised his, proposing a toast.

"To Margaret Forbes. May we carry her bold spirit with us always."

Blanche raised her glass too, but as she did, her eyes clouded with tears.

They touched glasses with a little ping. As Blanche set hers down, Frank reached out a gnarled but strong-looking hand and patted hers.

Then he looked around, taking in the thirty or so tables filled with residents in animated conversation. Coming to the dining room was the main opportunity for social interaction for many of them.

"I would venture to say that Miss Forbes is the subject of some of the discussion here this evening."

"Probably right," she said, following his glance. She appreciated him giving her the opportunity to regain her composure.

"People were a little awed by her—her personality, her outspokenness, her wealth, I suppose," Zanders said. "She must have seemed invulnerable to many."

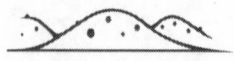

"None of those things matter in the end."

"Afraid not," Frank agreed. "We struggle all our lives and then poof, it's over. Evanescent." He pushed invisible air away with his hands.

Blanche nodded, making a mental note to look up evanescent.

Their conversation was lightened by the arrival of the salmon which lived up to its billing. A golden-brown puff pastry enclosed a thick pink fillet, and accompanying it was a wild rice dish with apricot compote. A dinner salad made up of fresh greens was served on the side, along with a basket of freshly baked focaccia.

"Can't beat it for the price," Zanders said, fork poised as he looked at the appetizing dinner in front of him.

"I thought price was no object for bankers."

Zanders laughed.

"Do you know how large her estate was?" She wondered how much Jack Forbes would be inheriting.

"About $30 million, give or take a couple hundred grand. She and her brother divided the profits when they sold out the family mining interests years ago."

"Albert?"

"Yes," he nodded, poised to put a large forkful of salmon into his mouth. "He left most of his money to a mining museum up in Chisholm."

"Nothing for Jack," she said.

"Nothing for the golden boy. That's why Margaret set him up at Quenton."

Blanche nodded. She knew the story from Margaret.

"Unfortunately Jack got her into some bad deals. He liked to trade a lot too, which cost her a bundle in commissions. She used to complain about it to me, and I told her,

`Hell, get yourself another broker. You don't owe him a living.'" Zanders was wiping his lips with the large linen napkin. He had finished every scrap of food on his plate.

"Dessert?" their waitress asked as she cleared their plates away.

Blanche asked for a cup of tea, needing something to draw out the dinner a little longer. Zanders ordered the chocolate layer cake.

"After this, Jack will really be living the high life, unless she changed her will again."

"What do you mean?"

"She changed it a couple of times," Zanders said. "I don't know the latest version."

"Why was she changing it?"

Frank shrugged his shoulders.

"You know Margaret. She'd get a bee in her bonnet about something and that would be that."

They'd finished eating and most of the other tables around them were empty.

"I don't know if I can move," Blanche said. "I don't know when I've eaten so much." She was grateful for the loose dress.

"I enjoyed the dinner very much," Frank told her in the lobby as they said good-night. "Let's do it again."

She was about to suggest that he come over to her place for a nightcap, but checked herself. Maybe he would think that was too forward. She would save it for next time.

She gave her hand to him and he patted it gently between both of his.

"See you at the service tomorrow," she said.

* * *

It was funny how long you could know someone, how much you could know about them, yet not really know them, Blanche thought as she walked towards her apartment. There were so many questions she'd like to ask Margaret now, so many things she wished they had talked more about.

"Mrs. Harriman, I'm glad to catch you."

She was startled by a voice behind her. She swung around to find it was Reverend Adams.

Blanche stopped, about ten feet from her door.

"I'm glad to see you've been mixing," he said with a knowing smile.

He must have seen her in the dining room with Frank, Blanche realized.

"I'm going to be conducting the service for Miss Forbes here tomorrow." He hesitated. "I know she wasn't a churchgoing person."

Blanche wrinkled her brow. What did he want?

"Well, the fact of the matter is, I don't know what she believed in. I thought you might be able to help me."

"She believed in truth," Blanche said, the words erupting from her as though she'd been waiting for an opportunity to use them.

"Truth?"

"Yes, truth and justice. She was a person of principle and passion and honor, and she fought for what she believed in." Blanche surprised herself with the rush of words.

"I see," Adams said, looking uncomfortable.

"She did not go gently, Reverend Adams, she did not go gently."

Before Adams could respond to that, Blanche turned away from him to her door. "Good night, Reverend," she said as she turned her key in the lock. She was aware he was staring after her. Let him try to work that into his service tomorrow, she thought with satisfaction.

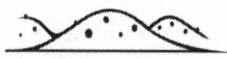

CHAPTER FOUR

"Truth and justice?" Reverend Adams mumbled aloud as he watched Blanche's door shut. What's she talking about? Confound it! He knew Margaret Forbes didn't like him. She must have talked with this brassy Harriman woman to make her come on so high-and-mighty like that! It caught him off guard and he didn't end up learning anything.

Adams had waited in La Mesa's front lobby for Blanche to come out from the dining room. His plan was to approach her casually and ask her some bogus question about Margaret Forbes' religious preference. What he really wanted to find out was whether Margaret had filled her ears with ruinous gossip about about the Masterson house. She'd refused to leave him alone about the house, always asking him when he was going to sell it and build his church. Damn it. It was no one else's business what he did with his own property. Peggy Masterson had left it to him.

Adams turned abruptly and strode past the front desk without even glancing at the night clerk. He got into his car, a late model Buick, dark green, and turned rapidly out of the parking lot. His home, the estate of the late Peggy Masterson, was across town near the top of Camino del Monte Sol. It was a jewel of a place set on three acres of magnificent Santa Fe real estate with show-stopper views in every direction.

Heading down the hill towards St. Francis Drive, he fished in the pocket of his Western-style sports jacket for a handkerchief to dab at the beads of perspiration which had formed on his forehead. It just might be that his problems weren't over yet. Margaret Forbes was out of the way, but what about this crazy Harriman woman? What if she took up the crusade? Christine Wilson told him they were very close friends.

At Canyon Road, he turned north, oblivious to the galleries and chic shops and the strolling couples enjoying the warm evening air. Farther along, he heard strains of classical music issuing from the area of The Compound, one of the city's finest restaurants. He braked slightly, thinking how superb the Oysters Rockefeller were. But they could be so snooty about dinner reservations, even to a man of the cloth.

To his right, just ahead, were three young women in shiny leggings and tight-fitting tank tops which accentuated every curvature of their bodies, even the nipples on their breasts. Did they have no shame at all? He watched them in the mirror after skirting around them.

At Camino del Monte Sol, he turned right, passing the gallery with the Nicolai Fechin painting he had his heart set on. It was a masterpiece of Modern Impressionism.

He had to come up with the money soon because they weren't going to hold it for him much longer.

Large clay pots overflowing with red geraniums lined the driveway leading to Adams' house. It never failed to please him to enter the serenely lovely property which he had acquired just six months ago as the result of a generous bequest left to him by Peggy Masterson, a wealthy widow who lived at La Mesa del Sol until the time of her death. Adams had cultivated her admiration and gained her sympathy for his idea of building a new church, and she had been most generous in leaving him her family home, worth over two million dollars on the Santa Fe market.

Of course she never expected him to live in it, but that didn't really matter now, did it? After all, he wasn't expected to live in abject poverty either. Reverend Adams smiled to himself, rocking back on the heels of his snakeskin boots, as he admired the flagstone floor which had been polished to a soft luster by Maria just that afternoon.

Now if it hadn't been for Margaret Forbes, he could have had a chunk of the Montoya estate too, he thought to himself. She was the most interfering, troublesome old bat he'd ever encountered. He didn't feel a drop of sympathy for the pain and terror she must have felt at the end.

Reverend Adams jerked his head around—an irrational gesture—as though he sensed someone might overhear his thoughts. Then he laughed aloud, knowing full well he was completely alone.

He noted with satisfaction that Maria had left lime slices and a full ice bucket on the counter in the kitchen. And yes, it was Crab Louie waiting for him in the warming oven! He poured Perrier over ice in a tall green glass and as he watched it bubble, he began to feel better. Things would

work out now. That Harriman woman was too feather-brained to be taken seriously by anyone. Margaret Forbes had been the real problem, and she was gone.

"Rest in peace," he said aloud, mockingly, as he raised his glass to the air.

CHAPTER FIVE

Blanche teetered in her three-inch black heels, contemplating the damage one false step could cause. But they were perfect with the black crepe shift which draped nearly to her ankles and gave her a stately look, fitting for a funeral. She'd walk carefully.

The black turban and attached veil covering her face was a more delicate issue.

"Do you think it's too much?" she asked Ruby Goldmark and Esther Zamora who'd come to collect her so they could go to Margaret's memorial service together.

"It's. . .very black," Esther said tentatively, trying to peer through the black netting.

"What do you think?" Blanche turned to Ruby.

"I don't think it's you." Subtlety was not one of Ruby's virtues.

"It doesn't have to be *me*. This is a funeral."

Ruby shrugged.

"You look fine, dear," Esther said.

Blanche plucked a bright-tangerine blossom off the potted azalea on her coffee table and pinned it to the tip of her V-shaped neckline.

"That's better," Ruby said approvingly as they went out the door.

* * *

They took their seats in the center section of the second-floor auditorium, close enough to view the speakers but not so far up front as to miss seeing who was in the crowd. People from "town" were expected because Margaret had been well-known in the community, and there was no way they would have all fit in the small chapel downstairs.

An usher handed them each a small card with a picture of a pale grey dove, its wings outstretched over a soft-looking cloud formation. On the reverse side was printed, "In Loving Memory of Margaret Rose Forbes". Then came a short prayer, "Be not severe in Thy judgment but let some drops of Thy precious blood fall upon the devouring flames."

Ruby turned to Blanche and raised one eyebrow meaningfully. "She'll come back to haunt whoever is responsible for this," she whispered.

Blanche snickered, a tad louder than she meant to.

The seats around them filled quickly. There was Elliot Gallegos from the State Board of Education, Esther whispered to Blanche, and just across the aisle from him, the current superintendent of the Santa Fe schools. Blanche caught sight of Helen Trinitsky positioning her wheelchair against the rear wall of the room. She was a retired librarian and now, despite being handicapped by the effects of a

stroke, volunteered in La Mesa's library. Blanche gave her a little wave.

Juanita Gomez was there too, sitting alone in the last row. If she saw Blanche, she did not acknowledge it.

Finally Jack Forbes came in, and Blanche was startled by the change in his appearance. The handsome, chiseled planes of his face had deepened into strained furrows and his color was pale beige tinged with yellow. He walked straight past them to the front of the room where he took a seat in the first row, next to Anthony Grace, administrator of La Mesa del Sol. Christine Wilson sat on the other side of Grace. Blanche recognized her by the smooth blond chignon.

Promptly at four, Reverend Adams entered the auditorium, looking very much like a funeral director in a black suit, white shirt and dark tie. He walked officiously up the aisle and then began a round of hand-shaking with Jack and the others sitting near him.

"His finest hour," Ruby whispered. "Probably the biggest audience he's ever had."

How ironical that it was all due to Margaret, Blanche thought. She would have had a fit if she knew!

Shortly, Adams walked over to a lectern which was flanked by two large vases of white lilies set on raised pedestals. He looked around at his temporary congregation— the auditorium seated 200 and it was nearly full—until all the whispering and shuffling quieted.

"Friends, we have gathered here today to pay tribute to Margaret Rose Forbes," Adams began, in dramatic intonations. "She was well-known by many of you as a strong voice in this community. . . perhaps some of you were even students of hers. . . of course that bespeaks a

different era. . . The youth of today are ignorant of the values which guided past generations. . ."

Adams' words began to wander across his favorite terrain and Blanche found herself tuning them out. Her eyes roamed over the crowd, picking out familiar heads here and there. This service was a charade and she felt strangely disloyal to Margaret for being a part of it. If she were up there watching from that soft cloud formation, she was probably getting ready to drop a bomb on all of them.

"The Lord hath great mercy, and we shall pray that he take mercy on her soul," Adams was saying.

Blanche's eyebrow went up.

Anthony Grace was next to approach the microphone. He was dressed like the Harvard graduate that he was, charcoal gray slacks, navy blue blazer, regimental tie.

"Those of us who knew and worked with Margaret Forbes found her a powerful force in our lives," he began, sounding vaguely like a commencement address. "We will miss that strong presence here at La Mesa. . ."

Ruby jabbed Blanche in the ribs with her elbow.

"Like hell he will," she whispered.

"Sssh," Esther warned.

Blanche's thoughts wandered again as Grace went on with platitudes about Margaret's service to the community. She was practicing saying the word "murder" in her mind. She was planning to talk with Ruby and Esther after the service. Maybe they'd know what Margaret had been up to. They'd all moved to La Mesa when it first opened and had been friends for years.

She thought about the possibility of Margaret being suffocated, but Christine said there were no signs of a struggle. Surely Margaret would have put up a good fight.

It could have been some sort of poison. A deadly poison that masked as a heart attack. Maybe some gruesome drug that worked slowly over time. Or chloroform. A chloroform-soaked rag held over her face.

She shivered.

"Are you all right dear?" Esther turned to her, her eyebrows wrinkled with concern.

Blanche nodded reassuringly and forced her thoughts back to her immediate surroundings.

Grace finished his remarks and Christine Wilson said a few words about what a vibrant spirit Margaret had been and that she was an example to everyone there. Then Frank Zanders came up, representing the La Mesa Resident Council. He sounded very impressive, Blanche thought, as he announced the purchase of a four-volume epic, *History of the Southwest,* for La Mesa's library in memory of Margaret. From where Blanche sat, she could hardly see the bald spot on top of his head.

There was a polite spatter of applause.

Adams closed the service with his reading of Psalm 129: "Eternal rest give unto her, O Lord, and let perpetual light shine upon her."

Those in attendance were invited to have tea and coffee in the rotunda, a large open lobby outside the auditorium. Serving tables had been set up next to the atrium which provided a lovely backdrop of flowering plants and greenery. Jack formed a one-man receiving line flanked loosely by some of the La Mesa administrative staff, as the mourners filed out.

"Jack, I am so truly sorry," Blanche said, extending a black-gloved hand.

"Thank you," he said without any sign of recognition.

Blanche planted herself in front of him before he could turn to the next person. "I don't know whether you remember me, Blanche Harriman."

"Oh, Mrs. Harriman, I didn't, ah, recognize you." He peered to get a look at her through the black veil.

"These are some friends of your aunt's, Esther Zamora and Ruby Goldmark."

While Jack shook hands, Blanche studied the dark circles under his eyes. He looked as though he hadn't slept for a week. She wouldn't have guessed that his aunt's death would have affected him so deeply.

"Will you be taking some time off of work to see to her affairs?" she asked.

"Well actually, I've left Quenton."

"Really?"

"I'm looking at other options, that's all." A red flush had spread across his face. Blanche could tell it wasn't a topic he wanted to explore further at the moment. Then he preempted any further conversation by turning away from her to accept sympathy from the next party.

"Mr. Personality," Ruby mumbled as they walked over to the refreshment table.

"Has he always been so communicative?" Esther asked sarcastically.

"I think he manages to find his voice when he wants something," Blanche said, reaching for one of the delicate praline cookies that La Mesa always served at special events. The table was decorated with freshly-cut roses grown year-round in the atrium.

"Mrs. Harriman. . .I am. . .so sorry." Helen Trinitsky had just wheeled herself up alongside Blanche. "She was. . .such a special. . .person."

Helen Trinitsky suffered from the effects of a stroke which had left her with a halting speech pattern and paralysis in her legs. There was nothing wrong with her mind though, Margaret had assured Blanche of that.

"Oh, please, call me Blanche." She slipped the veil up off her face so Helen could see her eyes.

"Saturday. . .I saw her. . .in the library."

"Oh?"

"She came in for . . .a book."

"A particular book?" The thought suddenly struck her that Margaret could have been researching whatever it was she was going to tell her about.

"Just. . .something. . .light. . ."

"Did she seem any different from usual?" Blanche hammered out the question.

Helen's heart-shaped face looked a bit quizzical. "No. . ."

"I was just wondering if anything might have struck you as out of the ordinary." Blanche thought she must sound like a special prosecutor to the three of them. Helen, Esther and Ruby were watching her closely.

"She usually read. . . history," Helen said. "But this time. . . she wanted. . . a novel."

"I see," Blanche said thoughtfully, wondering if the information was significant. She bit her bottom lip and got a faraway look in her eye.

"Something. . .wrong?" Ruby asked.

"Well, yes, as a matter of fact, there is."

The three women stared at her expectantly.

"I think we need to talk, all of us."

They waited.

"You see, I think that Margaret might have been"— she paused and glanced around before whispering—

"deliberately silenced."

There was a sharp, uniform intake of breath from the three women.

"What makes you say that?" Ruby demanded.

"I don't know if this is the best place to talk about it," Blanche said, indicating the milling crowd. "Could you come to my apartment tomorrow about one-thirty? I'll fill you in then."

Esther and Ruby glanced at each other, assessing this strange idea. "All right," they agreed.

"Helen?" Blanche asked.

Helen nodded. She'd be there too.

"I'll tell you everything I know about the situation then. We'll make it sort of. . . sort of a wake." The idea of a wake just popped into her mind. Sometimes those were her best ideas, the ones that came came to her like that, out of a blue.

Helen, Ruby and Esther barely had time to register their reactions to the idea of a wake because Anthony Grace walked up at that moment.

"My sympathy, Mrs. Harriman," he said, taking Blanche's hand. "Mrs. Goldmark. . . Mrs. Zamora. . . Mrs. Trinitsky," he added, turning to each of them. "This is a very sad occasion for all of you, I'm sure. I know you'll miss her a great deal." He patted Blanche's shoulder lightly before moving on.

"I wonder how much *he'll* miss her," Ruby said, sneering. "She was always on his case about something—the food service, the art in the lobby, the staffing of the health care unit—you name it."

"Critic-at-large?"

"More like `thorn in side'."

Blanche nodded. Yes, Margaret knew how to stick it to a person if she didn't like how he was handling something.

She saw Frank Zanders approaching just as she was about to slip out of her high heels. Her feet were killing her.

"How are you doing?" he smiled at her.

"Pretty well, considering the occasion," she smiled back. Just looking at him on the surface, he wasn't very attractive, she thought, taking in his paunch and thinning hair, yet he had a certain. . . *élan*. Maybe she should invite him to the wake too? No, she decided almost instantly, the women would be more comfortable talking by themselves, without a man around.

"Mrs. Harriman, how are we feeling today?" It was Christine Wilson.

"We are fine, I think," Blanche said.

"I was worried about you, with all the stress." Christine's pretty blue eyes showed her concern.

"I'm quite all right, really. You needn't worry." She was kind, almost excessively concerned, Blanche thought.

"You be sure and let me know if you need anything."

"Thanks, I will," Blanche said, distracted by Frank who was giving her a wink as he slipped off.

Shortly, the cookie supply dwindled, and people began to scatter. Blanche began edging away herself, saying a few passing hellos as she headed towards the elevator. She had turned down Ruby and Esther's invitation to join them for dinner because she'd decided there was something else she must do this evening.

It was another one of those ideas that had just come

to her in a flash. It seemed so obvious now, yet she'd only thought of it ten minutes ago. Inspiration came like that. One had to be open to all possibilities at all times, because you never knew exactly when the muses were going to speak.

CHAPTER SIX

Blanche sank her stocking feet into the plush, cream-colored carpeting of her living room, her high-heeled shoes abandoned nearby. She wouldn't have suffered like that for just anyone, she thought.

Then, taking three deep breaths to transition herself into a "new place"—a simple exercise encouraged by a former dance teacher—she padded to the bedroom to change clothes. She rummaged through a dresser drawer and found her green exercise tights and an oversized batik-printed T-shirt. Gratefully, she eased her feet into sequined hostess slippers, and tied a cranberry scarf gypsy-style around her hair. Pearl earrings were exchanged for large brass hoops.

In the kitchen she dug through her catch-all drawer to see what might be needed for this assignment, for that's how she already viewed it in her mind. It seemed so logical—why hadn't she thought of it before?

Plastic bags to collect evidence? She jammed a couple into her pocket. Gardening gloves? They'd be useful if something required special handling, and there'd be no fingerprints.

A wave of excitement passed through her.

The gloves gave her another idea. She'd put all the stuff in a basket with her snippers and gardening trowel. It was a perfect cover. If anyone wondered why she were prowling about the second floor, she'd say she was on her way to the atrium to snip back geraniums. Mrs. Medina, the volunteer in charge of the atrium garden, was always looking for help. She jammed her pocket copy of *The Complete Indoor Gardener* into the basket too.

And now, the key. She went to the little table just inside the front door where a single drawer held apartment keys, car keys, luggage keys, and various unidentified keys. When Blanche moved to La Mesa, she and Margaret had exchanged apartment keys as a precaution, in case one of them misplaced hers. She'd remembered about the key as she was leaving the memorial service. Now she reached into the back of the drawer and there it was, on the keyring from the Brown Palace Hotel in Denver where she and Arthur spent their 35th anniversary.

It was a few minutes after six. Most of the residents would be downstairs in the dining room or busy fixing dinner inside their own apartments, so the timing was good. The hallway was deserted. She stepped into the elevator and pressed the button for the second floor.

As she walked towards the rotunda, Blanche saw that the refreshment tables had been cleared away, and other than a few crumbs on the carpet, there was no sign of

the event held there such a short time ago. She swept her eyes across the south-facing glass wall of the atrium, marveling at the tumbles of red and pink geraniums, the roses, trailing ivy, and bursts of fuchsia bougainvillea. Certainly there must be some plant that needed pruning or plucking—she would claim that's what brought her back upstairs, in case she ran into someone unexpectedly, that is.

Margaret's apartment was four doors past the auditorium. Blanche stood outside her door for a few seconds to check the corridor. She could hear the muffled sounds of the six o'clock news coming from an apartment across the hall, but no one was in sight.

The solid wooden door opened smoothly before her as she turned the key. She stepped in and closed it quickly and quietly and found herself in semi-darkness, the postcard-perfect view of the Sangre de Cristo Mountains through Margaret's living room window now blocked by heavy drapes. They had watched so many sunsets together from here, the two of them waiting for that exact moment when the mountains were illuminated with iridescent pink light. It was one of the best apartments in the compound. When she moved here, Margaret told Blanche she "might as well live out her life in luxury."

Now though, the air was still and lifeless. Blanche tried to shake off the eerie sensation that something unexpected could be lurking in the shadows. She didn't know what she was looking for, but she hoped there might be some clue about what happened to Margaret on her last night.

Breathe normally, she reminded herself. You're just having a look around. Margaret wouldn't mind a bit. She

walked to the window to open the drapes part-way, causing a wedge-shaped pattern of light to flood across a fine old Persian rug. There, that was better.

She examined the familiar furniture, the antique tapestry love-seat, the small game table, the matching side chairs. She saw Margaret's white cardigan flung across a Spanish Colonial desk chair and had to resist an urge to pick it up and fold it neatly. Her eyes came to rest on the coffee table which held a book, a library book, she could tell from the marking on the spine. It was one of Tony Hillerman's Navajo mysteries. That was probably the book Margaret checked out on Saturday, she thought. She felt hot tears sting at her eyes but fought them back. She must not falter now.

She went into a small guest room to the left which Margaret had used for a study. Two shelves were completely lined with books, many of them educational texts. There was a comfortable-looking upholstered chair under a reading lamp, and an old-fashioned library table where Margaret worked. Papers were strewn across it, with more stacked in a wire basket on a shelf above.

Blanche scanned the papers on the desk. Catalogs, the usual junk mail, a personal solicitation letter from the Santa Fe Children's Museum, two postcards, a pharmacy bill, a large manila envelope, still sealed, from Quenton and Co. Not much different from the stack of mail on her own desk. She read the postcards. One was from someone named Caroline who was in New York seeing a different Broadway play every night. Another was from Hal and Grace Eaton, saying they were just thinking about her and wondering if she would be coming up to Denver this sum-

mer. She studied the bill from Walgreen's Pharmacy. It listed charges for a prescription drug called Omeprazole, 40 mg. The prescription had been filled on June 4.

Blanche turned her attention to the wire basket on the shelf over the desk. A copy of the "Regulations for New Mexico Nursing Homes and Long-Term Care Facilities" was on top, with a short cover letter dated May 29 and addressed to Margaret from the Office of John Rasmasson, Ph.D. She thumbed through the document, stiff with newness. Underneath was an assortment of news clippings, including two obituaries, one with a picture of Peggy Masterson, 75, a friend of Margaret's who had died at La Mesa in January, following surgery. Leland Strel, 74, another La Mesa resident, succumbed to pneumonia in April. Pneumonia, `the friend of the elderly,' Blanche thought ruefully. She remembered that Margaret had been very upset at losing two good friends within a few months of each other.

She'd make sure that the families of Peggy Masterson and Leland Strel were notified of Margaret's death, she promised herself as she put the clippings into her basket.

Blanche continued thumbing through the papers, mostly printed information and news clippings having to do with health care for the elderly. One yellowed clip from two years ago told of the drowning of an elderly resident in a nursing home in a small town in Colorado. The case had received national attention.

She left the study and walked towards the bedroom, aware of a knot in her stomach. Christine Wilson said they'd found Margaret on the bedroom floor, still in her dinner dress. Now Blanche studied the pale blue Chinese rug for some sign, but there was none. The bed was neatly

made, and a glance at the small bedside table and dresser top showed no indication of disorder. She tried to imagine Margaret coming in after the dinner with Jack, too distracted to concentrate on her book. She'd probably gone into the bathroom. Blanche traced the imagined steps and saw her cane, leaning in the corner.

On the bathroom counter was a jar of amber-colored mouthwash, a tube of clove-flavored toothpaste, dental floss, a bar of sandalwood soap in a cobalt blue soap dish. She studied the faint water spots on the pretty Mexican tile basin with its hummingbird and flower design. It didn't appear that Jack or anyone had been there yet to sort through Margaret's things.

She opened the medicine chest and took inventory. An expensive-looking face cream, skin toner, band-aids, various ointments and lotions, aspirin, ibuprofen, and a plastic prescription bottle. She picked up the bottle: Omeprazole, 40 mg., dated June 4, prescribed by Avery Hillman, M.D. a couple of weeks ago. It was nearly full of purple and white capsules. Blanche knew that Margaret had some stomach problems, possibly an ulcer stimulated by all the ibuprofen she took for her arthritis. That's probably why she had to take Omeprazole, she figured.

She was still holding the pill bottle, thinking about Margaret's arthritis, when she heard a funny sound. It was a door opening. Oh god, someone was coming into the apartment.

Soundlessly she slipped the bottle into her basket. She held her breath, straining to listen. Footsteps. . . in the kitchen? It sounded like the refrigerator being opened. There were no voices. Whoever it was, was alone.

Blanche's heart was pounding. It probably was someone from the staff. Or maybe Jack? How would she explain herself sneaking into the apartment like this? Would
they think she'd come to steal something?

Slowly, silently, she drew the bathroom door shut and
turned the small chrome lock just above the door handle.
It made a faint click, possibly enough to hear from the next
room, maybe not. She waited.

It was several long minutes before Blanche heard footsteps approaching Margaret's bedroom and bathroom. She
took silent, shallow breaths as she listened to the person in
the next room. A drawer was being opened, then shut.
There was the sound of something being set down on the
dresser. Then, steps approached the bathroom and someone was trying the door. The handle, just inches away, was
being jiggled furiously. She stopped breathing for long
seconds. Could they force it open?

"Damn!" She heard a man's voice curse. The rattling
stopped and she heard his footsteps retreating.

Blanche fought the urge to come out and announce
herself. She should have come out right away, she thought.
What a stupid thing to lock the door. Now it was too awkward to turn things around, pretend she wasn't *really* hiding. Her horse was right in the middle of the stream, as her
husband used to say.

She heard several short clicking sounds. . .the touch-
tone telephone? Then what sounded like a receiver being slammed into its cradle. After that, the footsteps went
back through the living room until she heard the front
door shut solidly.

Blanche thought quickly. He's likely to come back,
maybe with someone from housekeeping or maintenance,

with a master key to unlock the bathroom. She'd better get out of here fast.

She opened the bathroom door carefully and listened. The apartment was dead quiet again. As she stepped out, she reached back to draw the door shut behind her, wiping the doorknob with her t-shirt. She couldn't lock it from the outside, but at least it would look the same as before. Sometimes doors got stuck, she thought, trying to reassure herself.

Walking swiftly back through the bedroom and across the living room, Blanche hesitated for a split second at the coffee table, and then reached out for the library book and slipped it into her basket. She'd put it in the return slot at the library. On her way out she couldn't resist ducking into the kitchen and opening the refrigerator. She rapidly scanned the contents. Milk, cottage cheese, English muffins, a carton of eggs. She opened the cheese compartment: two chunks of cheese and a box of butter. Produce drawer—wilted lettuce and a single tomato. The shelves along the door held the usual—olives, mustard, mayonnaise, salsa, salad dressing, preserves. The freezer revealed two ice trays, a box of frozen waffles, some frozen vegetables. Nothing unusual. She wondered what the other visitor had been looking for, and whether he had found it.

At the front door Blanche listened; she couldn't hear anything outside. She opened it a crack and peered into the hallway. No one was in sight, so she stepped swiftly out, pulling the door shut behind her. It slammed firmly, making more noise than she intended.

She took four or five steps in the direction of the rotunda when she saw him—Reverend Adams—walking to-

wards her. Damn, he could have seen her coming out of the apartment; she couldn't be certain. Surely he'd heard the door shutting—the sound was still reverberating in Blanche's ears.

"Mrs. Harriman?" Adams said, as they neared each other in the rotunda.

"Good evening Reverend Adams," she responded, managing to sound calm despite the panic she felt inside. They were standing near the atrium.

"Anything wrong?"

Blanche shook her head. "Just came up to clip a few geraniums," she said. "I thought it would make me feel better to be doing something."

"Of course." Adams looked at her curiously.

"I'd better finish up before it gets too dark," Blanche said decisively. She walked past him and turned into the atrium. Out of the corner of her eye she could see him regarding her before he turned to walk on in the direction Blanche had just come from. She waited for a minute inside the atrium, and then slipped back out to look down the corridor and see where he was going. Maybe he was the man who'd gone into Margaret's apartment. But she hadn't moved fast enough. Rats! Reverend Adams was nowhere in sight.

CHAPTER SEVEN

By the time Juanita arrived, Blanche had made curried crabmeat dip, lined up the green margarita glasses, and brought out the Haviland china, a wedding gift to her and Arthur more than 50 years ago. She'd called La Flora Linda to deliver a lavish, colorful bouquet—no white lilies, she'd specifically instructed.

"The *señora* is having guests?" Juanita asked, appraising the scene.

"Yes, it's going to be—well, a few of Miss Forbes' friends are coming by this afternoon."

"Miss Forbes, she was a very special friend, no?"

"A very good friend, yes. We've known each other for many years."

"*Ah, si. Es muy difícil.*"

"Difficult indeed," Blanche said, arranging yellow cocktail napkins in a fan pattern. She looked at Juanita. "Did you notice anything *extraño*—unusual—about Miss

Forbes recently?" she asked.   Juanita had helped Margaret
with small tasks several times a week.

"What do you mean?"

"Anything out of the ordinary?"

"*No, nada.*"

"You could have overheard something. . .a telephone
call, an argument with someone?" Blanche prodded.

"*No, señora.*" Juanita shook her head firmly.

"Let me know if anything occurs to you," she said,
reaching into her pocket for the grocery list she'd begun
earlier.   "Now, let's see what I need.   Half a dozen limes,
two quarts of salt-free soda, three avocados, a bag of blue
corn tortilla chips, a bottle of Margarita mix, and a dozen
pastries from the French bakery," she read aloud.   "Have I
missed anything?"

Juanita looked a little uncertain.

"You'd better get some regular things too, I guess.   How
about some vegetables?   Carrots, zucchini, tomatoes, lettuce.   Some fruit, whatever looks good.   And get a couple
more of those frozen gourmet dinners."

"*Si, señora.*"

"Oh, I'm out of bread too.   Get me two of those nice
baguettes when you're at the bakery."

Juanita nodded, scribbling furiously.

"I'll finish up here and get myself together while you're
doing the marketing."

* * *

Ruby and Esther arrived first, promptly at one-thirty, and
Blanche, dressed up in a flowing emerald caftan, opened
her door like Loretta Young swishing in royalty.   The rich

green set off her wild henna curls in a dramatic way. It would be a terrific ensemble to wear, say, to opening night of the Santa Fe Opera, she thought as she appraised herself in the mirror.

"Come in, come in," she said, enthusiastically ushering them into the living room.

Esther looked a bit startled by the green caftan. Her style was more understated, linen slacks, creamy silk blazer, silver-streaked hair swept up in a perfect French knot. She was the widow of Franklin Zamora, State Land Commissioner for many years. Ruby Goldmark was large and horsey. She'd retired to La Mesa from New York City where she'd been a buyer for a line of high-end women's clothing. Her outfits were loose and flowing, with ethnic overtones, and accented by heavy silver jewelry collected on trips around the world. She divorced a philandering husband many years ago and—as she told Margaret who later reported it to Blanche—made him pay a heavy financial price for his misdeeds.

They were an unusual pair, linked by their common friend, Margaret. Blanche watched them look around tentatively before choosing the sofa. They each took an end. As soon as they were settled, there was a light tap-tap on the door. It was Helen Trinitsky, who couldn't reach the door-chime from her position in the wheelchair.

"Come in, come in, to our den of sin," Blanche welcomed her merrily.

"Thank. . . you," Helen said, a bit bewildered-looking as Blanche helped guide her wheelchair into the room. She was a small woman with short curly grey hair and gold-rimmed bifocals. A navy dress with a small white col-

lar and little pearl buttons down the front made her look sweet and demure.

"I've made up a pitcher of Margaritas," Blanche said. "What will it be, regular or virgin?"

Esther looked at Ruby.

"Regular," Ruby said. "After all, this is a wake."

"All right, I'll have one too," Esther said.

"Helen?"

Helen looked confused.

"Virgin—that means no alcohol," Blanche explained.

Helen's eyes crinkled with amusement. "I'm. . . no. . . virgin," she said in the hesitant speech which, along with her crippling physical condition, was the irksome evidence of her stroke.

The three women were laughing as Blanche glided off to pour their drinks into frosted Margarita glasses. She decorated them with pink paper parasols stuck into slices of lime.

"Here's to our own dear Margarita," she said, raising her glass in a toast.

"To Margaret," the others said, solemnly tapping their glasses together. Blanche thought everyone relaxed a little as they took a sip. It wasn't the alcohol, she knew, because she'd only used half a jigger of tequila for each drink. But toasting Margaret like this, creating a little ceremony, seemed to draw the women together.

"It was good of you to do this," Esther said, dipping a blue corn chip into the curried crab dip. "It's comforting to be together."

"I think Margaret would approve," Blanche said. "I know she wouldn't want us moping endlessly."

"You have something to tell us though, " Ruby said, moving directly to the point. "At the memorial service you said. . . well, you suggested someone may have done something to 'silence' her. What were you talking about?"

"Well," Blanche began, stopping to take a sip of her drink. "I don't believe Margaret died from natural causes. For one thing, she didn't have any problems with her heart, so I think it's odd that they're calling it a heart attack." Then, taking pains to sound matter-of-fact and rational, she explained how Margaret had been investigating something very strange going on at La Mesa. "I believe her investigation could have put her life in jeopardy."

"Something strange going on here??" Esther and Ruby reacted simultaneously. "What did she mean?"

"That's the problem. I don't know," Blanche said, raising her hands in mock defense. "She was going to tell me about it over breakfast on Monday morning, but that never happened. She said she had one more thing to do, or one more thing to get, before giving me the details. Then she said, she was going to need my help. That's the part that tells me it was serious. You all knew Margaret well enough to know she didn't usually need help with anything. It was a point of pride with her."

The three women glanced at each other and back at Blanche, but no one spoke immediately. Blanche continued, telling them how she had taken her theory to Christine Wilson and to Jack, and—this ought to convince them I'm not taking this lightly, she thought—how she'd gone to the police.

"You went to the police?" Esther's eyes opened wide.

"It seemed the logical thing to do, considering the circumstances."

"Well, what did they say?" Ruby demanded.

"The officer who spoke with me, Lieutenant Otero, basically advised me to seek counseling. He thought I was in the early stages of senility."

"Naturally," Ruby said. "Surprised they didn't offer to drive you home."

They all laughed.

"Seriously though, do any of you have any ideas about what Margaret wanted to tell me Monday morning? Was she involved in something here that I don't know about?" For the moment, Blanche didn't mention snooping around her apartment. They might consider that a bit improper, and right now she was trying to earn their trust.

"Well, there's the health care campaign," Esther said after thinking a minute.

"The what?" Blanche asked.

"Margaret always hounded that inspector—what's his name—Rasmasson, the state nursing home inspector, when he came here for monthly inspections. She had some way of finding out the date, and then she would just 'happen to be' in the health care wing while he was there. She would follow him around, asking him questions about new regulations and pointing out things that she thought weren't being done right. Ruby and I used to tease her about conducting her own campaign."

Blanche remembered seeing Rasmasson's name on a letter to Margaret, clipped to the copy of some new regulations.

"Actually, I have news to report," Ruby said in a way that riveted all attention on her. "Today was inspection day over in the health care wing and I just *happened* to have business there all morning."

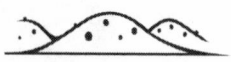

"You went through with it!" Esther exclaimed.

"I knew Margaret planned to be over there today asking him about the new restraint regulations for wheelchairs," Ruby said. "I didn't really know much about the regulations except for what she told me, but I decided to question him a bit anyway. You know. . . I did it for Margaret." She laughed.

"Ruby, how inspiring!" Blanche said enthusiastically. "What happened?"

"Not much, really. I got the mobile library cart and started wheeling it around. Most of the people over there are too sick to read, so I just strolled up and down the hall with it until I saw Rasmasson come in. Then I sauntered over to him as casually as I could and said, `Inspector, what about those new restraint regulations? I haven't seen a patient released from a wheelchair all morning.'"

They laughed.

"What did he say?"

"He looked surprised as hell," Ruby said, glancing at Esther, who never swore. "He mumbled something about how he would be reviewing all the charts to make sure we're in compliance."

"Margaret would be proud of you," Blanche said.

"Well we can't let all her good work go down the drain, can we?"

"Was she extra-worried about something over there?" Blanche asked, passing the guacamole.

Ruby shrugged. "No more than usual."

"She has seemed pretty uptight lately though," Esther said. "She hasn't played gin rummy with us for the past two Fridays."

"True," Ruby agreed. "I figured it was her arthritis kicking up."

"It's funny—she never talked to me about her concerns with the health care wing," Blanche said.

"She probably didn't. . . want to. . . upset you," Helen said. "You were. . . new here and all."

"Helen's right," Esther said. "All this started up around the time you were moving in. Margaret even told me she hoped she'd done the right thing in convincing you to come here."

"Did she take her concerns to the administration?"

"Anthony Grace? Oh, sure, he'd give her lip service," Ruby said. "But he didn't seem to change anything. Margaret thought he was more interested in his own image than in anything else. They had some real battles."

"So that's what you meant at the service yesterday, that Grace wasn't really going to miss her?"

"It's probably a relief to him to have her out of his hair," Ruby said.

Blanche poured coffee and passed the silver tray filled with dainty French pastries.

"Oh, I shouldn't, but I will," Ruby said, selecting a miniature creme puff glazed with chocolate. Esther and Helen took petits-fours decorated with tiny pink rosebuds.

"Was she involved in anything else you know about?"

"Well, there was Reverend Adams," Ruby said. "She thought he was milking all the lonely widows here." She looked around meaningfully at Blanche, Esther and Helen, all of whom were widows, before adding, "Present company excluded of course."

"Like the way he talked Peggy Masterson into leaving him that big house of hers," Esther added. "He was sup-

posed to sell it and use the proceeds for his church, but he doesn't seem to be moving on it very fast, does he?"

"He sure is sitting pretty up there," Ruby said.

"You can say that again," Esther agreed.

"He sure is sitting pretty up there," Ruby repeated.

"Oh Ruby, please, you're getting worse!"

Margaret hadn't made any secret of her feelings towards Reverend Adams. Blanche remembered the crack she'd made about him collecting stray bank accounts. "Isn't he obligated to sell it?" she asked.

"Not by law—they just had an understanding about it—or I should say Peggy had an understanding about it," Ruby said. "Obviously Adams has his own understanding."

"Margaret. . . questioned. . . the arrangement," Helen said.

"She'd take every opportunity to remind him that Peggy left him the property for his church, not for wallowing in a life of personal luxury," Ruby elaborated.

Helen nodded in agreement.

"Maybe I ought to take up where she left off," Blanche said. "Just to make sure he doesn't get too content."

"Put your armor on," Ruby warned. "He may look mild, but he can get downright nasty."

"Did Margaret have a will?" Esther asked.

"Yes, of course," Blanche said.

They all turned to her expectantly.

"Well, actually, I haven't seen it," she said. "I just heard about it. Frank Zanders mentioned it the other day." Blanche was coiling and uncoiling a curl with her finger.

"We saw you talking with him in the dining room," Esther said in a way that signaled Blanche she'd been observed closely.

"So what did he say?" Ruby wanted to know.

"Actually, he said she changed her will from time to time. He didn't really know where things stood when she died."

"I suppose her nephew—Mr Personality—gets most of it," Ruby said.

"He'll be needing it," Esther said.

They all looked at her.

"Oh, I heard him say those things about quitting his job, but I know the real story."

"Well, tell!" Blanche ordered. It was amusing to see Esther, usually so composed and mannered, just bursting to pass on a bit of good gossip.

"My granddaughter, Mindy, dates Alan Forrester, a friend of Jack's," she said, relishing her insider information. "Alan told Mindy that Margaret was Jack's only significant client. He had no choice but to leave once she was gone. He couldn't have earned enough to live on without her business."

So, Margaret *had* been supporting Jack in effect, Blanche thought.

"Actually—and this shouldn't be repeated," Esther began, lowering her voice. "The word is that Margaret was moving her account out of Quenton because she was so disappointed with Jack's handling of her investments."

"Really? When was that supposed to happen?" Blanche asked.

"Soon. She asked for the transfer papers last week."

The papers could have been in the manila envelope from Quenton and Co. that she'd seen on Margaret's desk, Blanche thought.

"Well, he won't have to worry about making a living from any of that now," Ruby said. "He's probably inherited a bunch."

"If she didn't write him out of her will," Blanche said.

"She was one tough lady," Ruby said respectfully.

"Maybe too tough for her own good," Blanche said.

The party broke up around four. Esther was meeting her son and daughter-in-law for dinner and wanted to take a short nap first. Helen had a meeting of the Territorial Book Club. Ruby said she was going to take the evening off and watch T.V.

"Maybe you could ask Dr. Hillman a little more about how she died," Esther suggested as they were standing in the doorway on their way out. "He might be able to tell you something. The idea of Margaret being, well, murdered, is. . . well, I don't know. . ." A blush began to color Esther's face.

"Hillman won't tell you much. The oath of Hippocrates and all that," Ruby interjected. "They can't talk about their patients."

Blanche knew doctors weren't allowed to discuss their patients with others, except for family members. But there could be ways around it. Maybe she could cook up an idea for getting information from Dr. Hillman without sounding too obvious about it.

* * *

Blanche was picking up the glasses and dessert plates when she noticed Margaret's library book on the coffee table. She'd meant to give it to Helen to take back. Now she picked it up and flipped through the pages.

A piece of paper, probably being used for a bookmark, was stuck about a third of the way into the book.

How curious, Blanche thought as she removed the paper. It was a list of names written in ink in a careful script that she didn't recognize. Next to some of the names, notations had been scribbled in pencil. The pencilled notes looked like Margaret's writing. One name, Sylvia Richards Bell, a person Blanche had heard of but didn't know, was underlined. Tomás Morales had a question mark. Two names were very familiar because she'd read them just last night in the obituaries on Margaret's desk—Peggy Masterson and Leland Strel. They both had "none" scrawled next to them.

The list read as follows:

Leland Strel   *none*
Margaret (Peggy) Masterson   *none*
Lenore Richards   *here*
Reginald Salazar   *here*
Rose Kay Armijo   *away*
Sylvia Richards Bell   *none*
Mr. and Mrs. Bud Rosenblum (Mary)   *here*
Adrian W. Curtis   *none*
Merilee Jamison   *away*
Tomás Morales   ?

Blanche went to her desk where she'd left her gardening basket. She found the two obituaries and put on her reading glasses. Peggy Masterson's told about her painting career, and named several awards she'd won. It said she was the widow of Wilfred Masterson, a wealthy Santa Fe real estate developer. Leland Strel's obituary recapped

his business career as local distributor for Agua Fria, a water purification system. He was an amateur photographer. The article didn't mention a wife or family. He'd lived at La Mesa for the past six years, about the same as Margaret.

She turned back to the list. She'd met a few of the others through Margaret, like Lenore Richards and Mary and Bud Rosenblum. She didn't know the rest, although some of the names sounded familiar. The underlining of Sylvia Bell's name made her feel strangely uncomfortable, she was aware, but she couldn't have explained why.

Well, she'd sleep on it, she decided. Right now she'd finish stacking the dishwasher and put the leftovers away. It had been a full day and she'd learned some interesting information about Margaret. And it had felt good to be with the other women who'd been close to her. She hoped she'd see more of them. Ruby was a riot, so opposite of Esther with her ladylike manners. And Helen was a constant and delightful surprise. People tended to dismiss her as a bumbling old lady because of her speech problem, but it was clear there was nothing wrong with her mind. They were quite a group.

She put the obituary clippings and list of names in the vegetable bin of her refrigerator, underneath the string of pearls tucked in a satin bag that Arthur had given her on their wedding day. She didn't know what the list meant, but she had a feeling it was significant.

As an afterthought, she got the prescription bottle she'd taken from Margaret's apartment and added it to the vegetable bin. No sense having someone come across it in her apartment. That would take some explaining.

CHAPTER EIGHT

Dr. Hillman was poring over papers on his desk when his receptionist showed Blanche into the office. He looked a little like Gregory Peck, she thought, noting the cleft chin, the distinguished touch of silver at his temples. The walls were bedecked with various medical degrees and certificates, and a striking black and red Navajo rug with the caduceus design, the physician's symbol of a staff with two intertwined snakes, hung behind his large desk.

"Ah, Mrs. Harriman, come in," he said, taking off his reading glasses as he looked up.

"I appreciate your taking time to meet with me like this," Blanche said.

"My pleasure. Please, have a seat." He gestured towards two leather chairs in front of his desk, revealing a glimpse of gold cufflink underneath his white coat sleeve as he moved his arm. "What can I do for you this morning?"

"I'm having these terrible forgetful spells," she said, with a practiced edge of anxiety in her voice. "Sometimes

I forget what I'm talking about right in the middle of a sentence." She paused to frown. "It has me worried."

"Is this a recent occurrence?"

"Relatively recent, yes, I would say."

"Since you moved to La Mesa del Sol?"

"Hmmmm. . .it probably was just around that time," Blanche said uncertainly. "It's difficult to say for sure—that's the problem, you see. I can't remember."

"I've looked over your admission form, which includes your most recent physical, the one you submitted from. . ." He paused to check the papers on his desk. "From Birch, Minnesota," he finished. "Looks like you're in pretty good shape."

"Well. . ." Blanche had planned to take on a vague look, and even express confusion about what she was doing in the doctor's office, but she was finding it difficult. Dr. Hillman was very handsome.

"Really, Mrs. Harriman, I don't think you have anything to worry about. It happens to all of us around this age." He smiled winningly as he put himself into her age category, but in fact, she'd doubted he could be over 60.

"I'm afraid I might wake up one morning and have forgotten my name."

"Do you have family here, Mrs. Harriman?" Hillman's tone was kindly, indulgent.

"I have one daughter, but she's not here. She lives in Phoenix."

"Are you currently taking any medication?"

"No. . .well, except for my blood pressure pill. I've taken that for years."

"Have you been under particular stress recently?"

"Well, yes, I guess you could say that I have." She tried to make it sound as though the thought had just occurred to her, but in fact, the conversation couldn't have been scripted better. She sighed deeply, seeming to struggle for composure. "You see, I lost a very good friend last week."

"Ah," he said, sympathetically.

"I just can't believe she's gone." Her voice cracked and she found tears filling her eyes. She wasn't play-acting now.

"I'm sorry," Hillman said, passing a box of tissues across the desk.

"It was Margaret Forbes," Blanche said, sniffling and dabbing at her eyes.

"Ah, yes, Miss Forbes."

"It was such a shock," Blanche said, blowing her nose as delicately as she could.

"It always is, no matter what the circumstances are."

"You were her doctor?" Blanche asked innocently, knowing full well that Margaret had been under Dr. Hillman's care for years.

"Yes, I was," Hillman nodded.

"I knew about her arthritis. But, I didn't know about her heart. What was wrong?"

"She had a little arrhythmia. We were watching it, and she knew she should take it easy but that's easier said than done, especially with Miss Forbes."

"Was she taking something for it?" she asked.

"Taking something?"

"You know, some medication."

"Mrs. Harriman, I really can't be discussing another patient with you unless you're a member of the family." Hillman's voice carried a hint of irritation. "But to answer your question, yes, Miss Forbes was under treatment."

"I know that patient records are confidential," Blanche said, dabbing at her nose again. "It's just that we were friends for such a long time."

"Now about you," Dr. Hillman said. "I would be pleased to take over as your physician here if you haven't already made other arrangements. Many residents find it's the most convenient way to handle things, but that is entirely your decision, of course."

Blanche nodded.

"You think about it. If you decide to transfer, we'll call Dr. Porter's office back in, let's see. . .Birch. . .and have your comprehensive health records sent out."

"All right."

"And in the meantime, we're available to you for any emergency, should it arise. You're welcome to get your flu shot here in the fall."

Blanche saw him look at his watch. "Well, doctor, I mustn't be taking up any more of your time," she said. "You've been very kind to talk with me."

"Not at all, Mrs. Harriman. It's been my pleasure."

Blanche's mind was whirling with thoughts as she left Hillman's office. Something didn't add up. She was positive Margaret would have said something to her about having a heart condition. Even if she didn't want to worry her, it would have come up sooner or later, like when they were talking about flying to Cozumel. The only reservation Margaret expressed about the trip was the possibility of her arthritis flaring up. Surely a heart condition would merit mentioning.

Dr. Hillman said they were "watching" her. Blanche got this funny picture of a room filled with doctors watch-

ing Margaret on a monitor. The fact that Hillman said they were "watching" suggested some sort of chronology to Margaret's condition, and who else was involved? He said *"they"* were watching. It would be interesting to see what notes Hillman might have attached to her medical record.

She wondered what kind of "treatment" had been prescribed. Was it the pills she took from Margaret's apartment?

Doctors have a way of excusing themselves when something goes unexpectedly wrong, Blanche thought as she let herself into her apartment. She'd love to have a look at Margaret's medical record herself and see exactly how serious Dr. Hillman considered this arrhythmia to be when he diagnosed it. He seemed to suggest it's the condition that led to her sudden death.

Underneath all of Blanche's rumination gnawed the irritating realization that people seemed to calmly accept Margaret's death as the natural course of events for someone eighty-two years old. Well, wait until they got there, she said aloud to herself. Then see how natural it feels.

* * *

Darn! Someone was knocking at the door while Blanche had a shower cap scotch-taped to her head and an old towel around her neck to keep the henna rinse from dripping down and staining her face. She had to leave the henna in for twenty minutes. Who could be knocking in the middle of a Friday afternoon? Obviously she wasn't expecting company. She peered through the peephole of her front door and saw the smooth, pretty face of Christine Wilson.

"I was just wanted to make sure you were doing all right," Christine said as Blanche opened the door a crack.

"You'll have to excuse my appearance. I was in the middle of a treatment."

"Oh, I won't stay," Christine said, eyeing the head wrap with curiosity. "Just dropped by to say hello."

"Despite what meets your eyes, I'm fine," Blanche said as she pressed the scotch tape close to her face.

Christine laughed. "I'm getting mine done right after work."

"Something special going on this weekend?" Blanche opened the door a crack wider.

"Sort of, I guess," Christine said. The color rose in her cheeks. "I'm going to a banquet with Anthony Grace."

"Oh? What's the occasion?"

"The New Mexico Business Association is honoring him, a tribute for what he's done here at La Mesa."

"Wonderful," Blanche said. "A young man on the move."

"His picture is on the cover of the *Business Journal* this month with a big article about La Mesa being the flagship institution of Esteem Enterprises."

"The flagship institution?"

"You know, the star among a chain of retirement centers they operate across the Southwest—California, Arizona, Texas, New Mexico."

"Quite impressive." Blanche dabbed at her left cheek with a tissue she found in the pocket of her shift. She could feel a trickle of henna rinse seeping down from her hairline.

"Well, I'd better scoot," Christine said. "Let me know if you need anything."

"Thanks," Blanche said, closing the door as Christine headed down the hall. In an instant she yanked the door back open.

"Wait," she called after Christine's departing figure.

Christine whirled around.

"Will Dr. Hillman be at the banquet tonight?"

"Oh, for sure!" Christine called back. "He's an important part of La Mesa's team."

* * *

Blanche was bent under the faucet of the stainless steel kitchen sink letting the warm water rinse through her henna hair until the color ran clear. An inkling of an idea was beginning to form in her mind. As she straightened and reached for her towel, she felt a flutter of excitement. Helen Trinitsky would be perfect!

"Helen, it's Blanche," she was saying into the telephone minutes later. "Something's come up and I need to talk with you." Her voice was urgent.

"What. . .what is it?" Helen sounded concerned. "Are you all. . .right?"

"I'm fine, but I need your help on a special project." Blanche was toweling her hair on one side while keeping the receiver pressed to the other. "I'd like to come over to your place and tell you about it. It has to do with Margaret Forbes," she added.

"Margaret?"

"Yes, Margaret. I'll fill you in when I get there." She wasn't going to give Helen a chance to refuse.

"But. . .what. . .?"

"Helen, I can't really get into it over the telephone. It's too important."

Blanche finished blowing her hair dry, using her fingers to twirl the red curls into a stylish tousle while she thought about Helen. She was smart. And she'd known Margaret for a long time which gave her a vested interest in the situation. She looked so innocent in her wheelchair with that stammering speech that no one would ever suspect her of doing anything devious! Now the only challenge was to convince her.

An hour later, Blanche was sitting on the flowered love seat in Helen's tidy living room.

"We need to get a look at Margaret Forbes' medical record," she told her.

Helen eyed her cautiously.

"You see, I don't believe she had a heart condition. I think Hillman is lying when he says she was under treatment for it, and I think I can prove it."

Helen's eyes widened. "What are. . .you. . .going to do?"

"What are *we* going to do," Blanche corrected. "This is where you come in."

Helen waited, wary.

"I've worked out a plan. The cleaning crew comes in every night to do the offices, right?"

"Clean. . .the offices?"

"The medical offices on the first floor." She pulled out a crudely drawn sketch of the area and leaned closer to Helen to show her. "Dr. Hillman's office is right across from the restroom," she said, pointing.

"I create a distraction in the restroom about nine-thirty and scream for help." Her index finger was on the square labelled toilet. "When the cleaning crew comes to

see what's the matter, I'll keep them busy while *you* wheel into Hillman's office." She moved her finger to the square marked Hillman.

Helen was staring at her like she'd lost her mind.

"I happen to know that Dr. Hillman is going to be at a banquet downtown tonight, so there's no chance of him showing up."

Helen's face was a bulletin board of questions.

"You just need to get into the patient file cabinet. I'm pretty sure it's right here." She scribbled an X for the approximate location of the two large steel file cabinets she noted when she was there. "It shouldn't take more than a minute to find Margaret's file and flip through it. See if there's anything written down about a heart condition."

Helen's eyes widened. "What. . .are you. . .trying. . ?"

"I want to know what records he's kept on her," Blanche said. "He says they've been watching this for some time, so that suggests there's be plenty of information in her file, right?"

Helen's head nodded slowly in assent.

"If there's *nothing* in there about a heart problem, then I'd like to ask the revered doctor a few more questions. I'd like to know why he's lying."

"Mal. . .practice?" Helen asked.

"Could be," Blanche said. "He may be covering up some mistake and figuring no one's going to notice. He figures no one's going to question her death because she was elderly." She bit her lip in frustration. "I don't know, but it just bugs me that Margaret never said anything."

Helen looked hesitant.

"We wouldn't be doing anything *that* wrong, you know,"

Blanche said. "We just want to have a look, and we want to do it before anything in her record gets altered."

Helen still didn't look too committed.

"Look, we need to move fast on this or it will just go down as quietly as a spring snowstorm," Blanche pressed. "After a day or two, everything melts and you never even know it happened. No one even thinks about it again."

"But. . .me?" Helen protested. "I'm. . .so. . ." Her voice trailed off as she indicated her wheelchair.

"Look, there's nothing wrong with the way your mind works," Blanche said, sounding like a drill sergeant giving a pep talk before shoving the troops out into the battlefield. "You're perfect for this because no one would ever suspect you of doing anything wrong. You're practically a saint around here."

"I. . .don't. . .know."

"Helen, I wouldn't have asked you if I didn't have full confidence in you."

Blanche startled herself with the sound of her own words. What was happening to her? What would they say back in Birch if they knew what she was about to do?

* * *

Shortly after nine o'clock that evening, Helen and Blanche left Helen's apartment together, heading towards Dr Hillman's office. Helen used the battery-operated control to move her wheelchair forward at a steady pace, while Blanche, carrying her secret cargo in a handwoven satchel on her shoulder, walked alongside. "If anything goes wrong, just play dumb," Blanche's last words of advice had

been to Helen before leaving the apartment. "The police will never arrest anyone in a wheelchair, especially if you stare at them with a glazed expression, like you don't know what you're doing."

Words of encouragement? Helen smiled tightly. She didn't know just how she'd allowed herself to be talked into this, but it was too late to turn back.

As they approached the front lobby, quiet at this time of evening, they looked around. J.J. Chavez, the night attendant, was perched at his concierge station next to the main entrance reading the sports section of *The Capital Times*. A woman whom Helen judged to be in her mid-twenties sat at the receptionist desk filing her nails and watching a small television set on the counter. She must have sensed them staring at her because she looked up.

"Good evening," Blanche said pleasantly.

"Hello ladies," the young woman said cheerfully. She smiled at them and resumed filing her nails.

Helen and Blanche proceeded past the entrance to the dining room, now closed, and continued to where the corridor jogged west towards La Mesa's administrative offices. They could hear the sound of a vacuum cleaner coming from down the hall. Just as they'd calculated, the cleaning crew was at work. Light shone from the open doorways of three offices on their right, including Dr. Hillman's.

Helen looked up at Blanche and nodded. She'd been right, Helen's nod acknowledged. The timing was perfect.

With a thumbs up gesture and a quick wink of one unusually bright eye, Blanche left Helen's side and began walking briskly down the corridor to the women's restroom. Helen wheeled herself just far enough down the

same corridor to be out of view by anyone in the lobby area and waited, noting the exact time on her wristwatch. Blanche told her she'd have ten minutes maximum to find the file. After straining to listen for several minutes, she heard the faint sound of the first toilet flushing, and then the second. Her heart was pounding. Finally Blanche burst loudly through the restroom door. Helen had to give it to her, the woman had nerve.

"My shoes! My best shoes are ruined!" Blanche called out the news dramatically as she stomped across the corridor to get the attention of the cleaning team, Mr. and Mrs. Martinez, a middle-aged Hispanic couple who worked evenings and weekends.

"There's a flood! My best shoes!" She wailed to a startled-looking Mrs. Martinez who stepped out of the middle office with a pink dusting cloth in her hand.

Mrs. Martinez followed Blanche into the restroom to see for herself what had happened. In seconds, she was back out and calling for her husband who was still running the vacuum next door in Dr. Hillman's office.

"Carlos, *pronto!*"

The sound of the vacuum cleaner stopped and Helen could hear a man's voice.

"*¿Que pasa?*"

"The toilets. They run over. Quick, get the mop."

"Ayee!" He ducked back into Hillman's office to retrieve a large rag mop and metal pail on wheels. Together Mr. and Mrs. Martinez charged into the restroom with Blanche right behind them still carrying on about her shoes.

As soon as the three had disappeared inside, Helen, with a glance behind her to make sure that no one was approaching, turned on the speed button on her wheelchair

and rapidly travelled the rest of the way down the hall. She moved directly to the open door of Dr. Hillman's suite, pausing only a second to listen to the excited voices coming from the bathroom, before entering the front office. Swiftly, she steered her chair around the vacuum cleaner which had been abandoned in the middle of the floor, and over to the two tall blue metal file cabinets which stood behind the receptionist's shining desk. Blanche's drawing of the floor plan of the office, gleaned from close observation during her appointment this morning, had not been in vain. Using the arms of the chair to ease herself up, she stood and opened the top drawer of the cabinet on her left. Her hands flipped swiftly through the file folders which, she learned, contained insurance information, billing forms, extra copies of a newsletter called "Staying Healthy in the Golden Years". Nothing there. She turned to the cabinet on her right and opened the top drawer. Her hands shook slightly as she flipped through the folders which were in alphabetical order by surname: Chavez. . . DeBaca. . .Desmond. . .Estes. . . Feinstein. . . Fenn. . . Franklin. . . Gonzales. . . She went back over the F's again, one by one. No Forbes. Shutting the drawer and opening the one underneath it, she found the alphabetized names had already reached the K's. She bit her lower lip as she concentrated on where to search next.

Helen sat back down in the wheelchair and pushed herself away from the file cabinets and out of the reception office towards Hillman's personal office located at the rear of the suite, across from two patient examining rooms. It was important to move swiftly, she reminded herself as she pushed on to Hillman's desk. Blanche said it wouldn't take

long for professionals like Mr. and Mrs. Martinez to clean up two overflowing toilets.

There were three stacks of papers on top of the dark mahogany desk. She checked through them swiftly and methodically. In one pile she saw Blanche's own medical records, the ones sent from Minnesota. But she found no folder with the name "Forbes" on it. Her eyes darted about the desktop which seemed to lack all the usual collection of memorabilia one was accustomed to seeing on office desks. No family pictures—Helen knew that Hillman was not married, no coffee mug with a funny saying on it, no hand-painted pencil jar made by some adoring niece or nephew. Only a lustrous black Indian pot from Santo Domingo Pueblo with a bear-claw design pressed into the front, and a gold pen in a holder shaped like a tall, slender iris.

Helen hesitated a split second before trying the middle desk drawer. Somehow, riffling through the papers on top seemed less incriminating than opening a closed drawer. Don't lose your nerve now, she told herself. Then, as she slipped her fingers underneath the catch, the wide drawer glided open and delivered its prize like a butler's tray offered to a royal guest.

She felt her heart pounding as she saw the dark green folder with Margaret Forbes' name attached. She opened it eagerly. On top of the stack of papers was a copy of a standard examination record, the type submitted to insurance companies, dated May 1. Dr. Hillman or his nurse had marked certain categories with a check, including "Physical Examination" and "Laboratory." A scribbled "110/85" had been written in next to "BP," blood pressure. Nothing

to be concerned about with a blood pressure like that—her own was probably running double that at the moment, she thought as she turned over the report and started to scan the next piece of paper. Suddenly she heard the sound of a shrill voice coming from the hallway.

"But what will I do about my shoes!" Blanche was saying loudly. "They're ruined!"

Helen closed the folder and crammed it into the side pocket of her wheelchair. She snapped the desk drawer shut, shoved herself away from it, and turned the wheels of her chair as fast as she could work them, forgetting all about the automatic speed control, until she got back to the outer office. She was breathing rapidly. Oh Lordy, don't have another stroke here, she told herself, taking a deep breath to try and calm her rapid heartbeat. She knew Mr. and Mrs. Martinez were in the hallway just outside and that Blanche was trying to stall them. They'd be back in the medical suite in a matter of seconds. From the way it sounded, they'd already finished mopping up the mess caused by Blanche jamming half a dozen sanitary napkins into two toilets and were ready to get back to their regular cleaning duties.

Quickly she assessed the possibilities. One way or the other, either inside Hillman's office or coming out of it, they were going to see her. She decided it would be better if she were coming out of it, so she wheeled herself right into their midst while Blanche was still trying heroically to distract them with her dripping white pumps which Helen happened to know she hated anyway.

"What. . . what happened?" Helen asked before anyone had a chance to question her. "I. . . heard. . . noises. . . saw

the lights." With this she gestured towards the open offices which were all lighted brightly. She furrowed her brow and tried to assume the confused expression Blanche had told her to use in case there was trouble.

"Everything is fine," Carlos' wife said reassuringly. "Two toilets, they overflowed. It is all taken care of." She glanced nervously at Blanche who stood in her stocking feet, wet shoes in her hands.

"My new pumps are ruined," Blanche said testily. "I'm going to hold La Mesa responsible for replacing them too."

Helen looked at Carlos and his wife with a bewildered expression and shook her head from side to side in sad sympathy for the situation.

Then Blanche, in her stocking feet and holding her wet shoes in one hand, abruptly took hold of the handles on Helen's wheelchair and turned it towards the lobby.

"Come dear, I'll see you back to your apartment," she said. Then, loudly enough for anyone in the area to hear, she added, "I never dreamed that stopping to powder my nose would turn into such a catastrophe!"

CHAPTER NINE

From Anthony Grace's condominium at Mountain Head, the horizon spread itself before him like the world's largest Dynamax movie screen. Pinon-dotted hills rolled up onto a wide sweeping plateau that led north to the rugged Jemez Mountains. Each day at sunset, the wispy strips of cirrus clouds hanging over this desert tableau, turned a startling flamingo pink, bringing gasps of pleasure from those lucky enough to be watching.

The view had been a selling point when Grace bought the condominium a year ago. But he didn't even think about it now except on those rare occasions when he was entertaining guests on the patio. He often worked late at La Mesa del Sol and then had dinner at a restaurant in town before driving out the Old Pecos Highway to the elegant complex known as Mountain Head. By the time he got home, sunsets were bedding down for the night.

Grace set his scotch on the dresser, putting the wet glass on an envelope so as not to mar the polished mahogany while he concentrated on tying his black bow tie. The formal tuxedo emphasized his heart-shaped boyish face, making him look younger than his thirty-eight years. He'd overheard someone at the Chamber of Commerce saying that he "looked like a kid" and he'd found it amusing.

Those old farts don't know their ass from first base, he thought. To them, opening another taco stand in Santa Fe was a big deal. He grinned in the mirror, relishing the image of himself as the young wizard.

Grace gathered up a clean linen handkerchief, wallet, and car keys and went downstairs through the chrome-accented living room to the attached garage where his white vintage Jaguar was parked. It never failed to give him pleasure to slip into the old classic which had been restored in Boston before he drove it out West. He was quite sure it was the only one like it in the entire state of New Mexico.

Inviting Christine Wilson to be his date for the banquet was a bit like a business arrangement, he supposed, as he backed out of the garage. But maybe it could evolve to something more. His invitation seemed to please her. She'd asked how formally she should dress.

He felt a shiver of anticipation at the thought of Christine Wilson dressing for him. She was a classy woman—he'd always seen that, but he hadn't allowed himself to mix pleasure with business until now. This was the perfect occasion. Christine Wilson could be very important to him.

He had no trouble finding her house on Upper Canyon Road and parked in front of the blue wooden gate as instructed. A tumble of color greeted him around the tidy

brick patio inside the gate. Clay pots filled with pansies, impatiens, and geraniums were tucked among blazing forsythia and fragrant Spanish broom. Grace took hold of the wrought iron door knocker and gave two knocks. He felt a twinge of. . .what? Nervousness? It had been months, maybe a year, since he'd been on a date. He was trying to build a business which didn't leave time to be wining and dining women.

"Hi," Christine said, smiling broadly as she opened the door.

"Hi," he swallowed. He was taken off guard by the dramatic change in her appearance. She looked like a Grecian goddess. Her smooth blond hair was swept up into an elegant twist, and her long, slim neck was graced by a single strand of large luminescent pearls. Her gown swished gently, folds of pale grey silk draping from one shoulder down over full breasts until being gathered in at the waist. "You look great," he added after a second.

"You like it?" She smiled coquettishly as she led him inside, twirling around so he could have the full effect. Obviously, she knew how well the dress suited her.

"Terrific." He had trouble peeling his eyes away from her bare shoulder.

"Thank you," she said appreciatively. "You look pretty fancy yourself," she added, sweeping her eyes over Grace's tuxedo.

He grinned.

"How about a drink before we go?" she asked, seeming in much more control than he was at the moment. "I'm afraid there aren't too many choices. . . white wine or scotch?"

"Scotch for me, on the rocks."

She fixed him the drink and poured wine for herself. He was walking around the living room examining the eclectic collection of paintings and Southwestern artifacts. No decorator's hand had been here, Grace recognized, yet the effect was pleasing.

"Nice place," he said.

"Thanks. I inherited most of the paintings from my grandparents. They picked them up for a song when they moved here in the `20's. Now you can't touch those painters from the Taos School unless you're a J.Paul Getty."

J.Paul Getty he knew about. The Taos School, he did not, so he just nodded in agreement. "I'd love to study them more closely sometime," he said, taking a long swallow of his drink.

They parked the Jag in the garage just east of La Fonda Hotel and walked around to the front entrance past a row of display windows filled with Indian pots and turquoise and silver jewelry. The Saturday night crowd, an avant-garde combination of funky and chic, milled around the lobby where a hostess in red fiesta dress and concho belt reigned like a queen over dinner reservations for the courtyard restaurant. A few Pueblo Indian women strolled about showing the *turistas* turquoise and silver earrings on black velvet-covered boards.

Grace took Christine's arm and steered her past the lobby crowd and the famous Gerald Cassidy paintings towards a banquet room in the rear, behind the restaurant and shops. There the atmosphere was relatively subdued, although probably a hundred people already had gathered. Most of the men were dressed in tuxedos, except for the Chamber of Commerce officials who wore their identify-

ing crimson jackets. The women's costumes ran the gamut of fashion statements, some hinting of exotic origin, others looking flowery and fragile, while some were brilliant and bold. The classic restraint of Christine's gown caused a few heads to turn as they entered the room.

"Mr. Grace, welcome," said one of the red jackets who'd been standing guard to await his arrival. He pumped Grace's hand as they stepped into the room and looked expectantly at Christine.

"This is Christine Wilson," Grace introduced her. "Director of Nursing at La Mesa."

The red jacket grinned leeringly at Christine as they shook hands. Grace steered her further into the room.

"Champagne?" a server asked as he stood before them holding a tray of glasses that brimmed with bubbly liquid.

Christine accepted, but Grace declined with a wave of his hand. He could feel the effects of the two scotches already and knew he could not afford to lose any control over his tongue or his judgment tonight. Under different circumstances, it might be fun to lose control and judgment, he thought, but not yet.

They were stopped by at least a dozen people as they edged their way towards the hors d'oeuvre table at the far end of the large room. He noted the admiring looks from the men and the appraising ones from the women as he introduced Christine.

"Miss Wilson, you're looking very lovely this evening," Dr. Avery Hillman said, giving her a peck on the cheek. "She's the most elegant woman here by a long shot," he said, winking at Grace.

Christine laughed with pleasure.

Eventually the guests began to take their seats and Grace and Christine were directed to theirs at the head table. A copy of the *New Mexico Business Journal* with Grace's picture on the cover, had been placed at each setting.

"This is terrific," Christine said as she leafed through her copy.

Grace smiled, trying to appear casual about how much it meant to him. Esteem Enterprises was going to be very happy about all of this. He must remember to have his secretary send several copies of the magazine to corporate headquarters. He'd already caught the attention of the marketing department with the life care annuity program, and now he was a cover story.

The Master of Ceremonies was beginning a rambling introduction to Anthony Grace, recipient of the Businessman of the Year Award. The attendees, now numbering well over a hundred, listened politely as the Chamber speaker cited Grace's accomplishments at La Mesa and its contributions, mostly financial, to a number of community organizations. They broke into applause when he called La Mesa "one of Santa Fe's new stars" and said there was a waiting list of people from all over the country who would like to retire there.

"You know, I wouldn't mind moving there myself...how old do you have to be?" the Chamber official, a heavy-set, florid-faced man in his early fifties, asked as he turned to Grace. The crowd laughed politely.

Grace smiled evenly.

The red carpet continued to roll, with laudatory remarks from two or three other community groups, including the "*Conquistadores*", a local service club who took

their name from the Spanish soldiers who conquered Santa Fe in 1610. They presented Grace with a bronze medal, making him an "ambassador" to "*Nuevo Mexico*".

When it was all over, and his hand was feeling the effects of countless congratulatory shakes, he steered Christine back out into the lobby. "How about a quiet drink somewhere?" he asked.

"Sounds wonderful," she said, smiling up at him.

* * *

Sitting across from her at a little table in the bar at La Posada as they waited for their drinks, Grace felt a bit awkward. "I guess La Mesa del Sol is getting on the map," he said, trying to appear casual.

"I'd say it's already there," Christine said, smiling. "By the sound of it, you'll have to build another wing to accommodate everyone on the waiting list."

"Well, not immediately," he laughed. "The turnover is pretty good."

Christine looked puzzled for a second and then caught his meaning. "Oh," she said.

"Sorry," he said, making a goofy face. "It's the nature of retirement communities. Average life spans and all."

The waitress was placing a brandy snifter with *Gran Marnier* before Christine, and one with *Courvoisier* in front of Grace.

"I know," Christine resumed sadly. "That's the hardest part of this business. We lost a very special lady just last week."

Grace frowned. "Who was that?"

"Margaret Forbes."

"Oh yes, of course."

"She was so feisty—I'll miss her," Christine said, taking a sip of the pungent orange liqueur and allowing it to roll over her tongue where it produced a pleasant prickling sensation.

"She may have been feisty, but she was also over eighty. Being feisty can't get you past that reality."

"She was in good shape though," Christine said.

"Bad heart," Grace reminded her.

"Her friend Blanche Harriman doesn't think. . ." She hesitated.

"What?"

"Oh, it's sort of silly."

"Come on."

"Do you know Mrs. Harriman? She moved here about six months ago, a close friend of Margaret Forbes."

"Is she the flashy redhead on the first floor?"

"Well, I don't know that I'd call her that," Christine said protectively. "Anyway, she told me Margaret was supposed to meet with her the day she died."

Grace took a swig of the cognac.

"She said Margaret was going to tell her about some strange goings-on at La Mesa, but of course Margaret never showed up. Mrs. Harriman thinks her death may have been connected to whatever was going on, that someone may have wanted to keep her quiet about it. She went so far as to suggest that Miss Forbes may not have died from a heart attack."

Grace screwed up his face in disbelief.

"Oh, it's all sort of vague," Christine said, waving her hand as though it were indeed too much to consider. "She's

convinced that Miss Forbes never had a heart problem. She was even asking about an autopsy."

"That's wild. What did you tell her?"

"That there was no call for it, of course. But she's very serious. I'm a little worried about her."

"What got her going on all this?"

Christine shook her head. "I think it's a case of classic psychological denial. Too hard to accept the truth of her friend's death, so she builds up a different scenario."

"Is she. . .unstable?"

"Blanche? Oh no, I don't think so. She's just upset."

"Keep an eye on her. We don't want any loonies making trouble around the place."

Grace regretted his choice of words when he saw the hurt register in Christine's eyes. "Sorry," he said more gently. "I just don't want her imagining all sorts of crazy stuff and upsetting the other residents."

"I know," Christine said.

"You look beautiful tonight," Grace said then. He fixed his eyes steadily on hers until, flustered, she had to look away.

CHAPTER TEN

"You were out last night." It was nine o'clock in the morning and Mitzi was calling from Phoenix.

"Well, I've reached the age of consent, you know," Blanche said, sipping her coffee.

"I tried to reach you half a dozen times. Where were you?"

"I spent the evening with a friend." Blanche smiled as she said it, picturing Mitzi's reaction if she were to tell her she'd been out jamming toilets in order to orchestrate a break-in to Dr. Hillman's office.

"Male or female?"

"Oh, Mitzi, really. I was with Helen Trinitsky, an old friend of Margaret's who used to work for the schools here. She's a librarian and she's had a stroke. People treat her like some kind of oddity because she has trouble talking. She's a lovely person."

"Well, that's nice," Mitzi said. "I'm glad you're making friends. I've been thinking about you all week. How was the funeral?"

"A ceremony of platitudes. Everyone made a lot of glowing remarks about Margaret, most of them absolute bull."

"Mother, really."

"I'm serious," Blanche said. "Some people are probably glad to see her gone. I'm sure Jack isn't too broken up about it. They didn't have what you call a close relationship. She was on the verge of withdrawing her account from Quentin when she died."

"No kidding. How come?"

"He kept losing money for her."

"So what will he do now that she's gone?"

"Probably just wait for his inheritance to roll in."

"Poor guy."

"*Poor* is not exactly the word I would use," Blanche said.

"She left him quite a chunk, huh?"

"Considering it's a thirty-million-dollar estate and he's the only living relative, I'm sure he'll get a nice little something."

Mitzi let out a long whistle. "Wow, that's what she was worth, huh?"

"That's what Frank Zanders told me."

"Who's Frank Zanders?"

"He's a retired banker. He lives here."

"Hmmm," Mitzi said as though she'd just unlocked a secret. "So, how are you doing through all this?"

"It's been a hard week, but I'm all right," Blanche said.

"I could fly over for a visit when the kids go to summer camp."

"I thought you and Jim were going to San Francisco?" This was a new twist, Blanche thought. Mitzi was being solicitous.

"Well, we were planning to," Mitzi said. "But we could scratch those plans in a minute if you'd like me to come spend some time with you."

Blanche clutched. That's the last thing in the world she needed right now. "I'm fine, really," she urged. "Don't worry."

"Well, I do, you know."

"Well you can relax, dear. I'm perfectly all right."

As she hung up the receiver, she sat for a minute, thinking she had detected a real note of concern coming through Mitzi's usually distracted voice. It surprised her. They didn't enjoy one of those chummy mother-daughter relationships. They viewed the world so differently that Blanche had learned to limit her conversation to superficial topics which kept them on safe, non-confrontational ground. Now here was Mitzi, proposing to give up her summer vacation to come visit her.

"What have I done to deserve this?" she wondered aloud.

* * *

Blanche turned her attention back to Margaret Forbes' medical file, the contents of which were spread out before her on the kitchen table. She and Helen had gone through the papers last night but found nothing to indicate that Dr. Hillman was treating Margaret for a heart condition.

Helen could have gotten an Academy Award for her performance! Blanche laughed aloud as she thought of the dazed look she'd managed to put on as she came wheeling out of Hillman's suite. Blanche didn't realize until they got

back to Helen's apartment that she'd taken Margaret's file with her.

The thing was, as Helen explained in her halting speech, there wasn't time to read it on the spot when she found it in Dr Hillman's desk drawer. She *had* to take it with her. After a glass of sherry, Blanche decided it wasn't a criminal act. They were just borrowing it.

But now, with a cup of strong coffee to help her focus, the idea of taking the file made her a bit uneasy. Blanche flipped through the papers again. There were half a dozen completed examination forms, a chart tracking weight and blood pressure, a few scribbled notes about swelling in knuckles and knee joints and pain in left shoulder, plus records of prescriptions which Dr. Hillman had written for Margaret over the past three years.

No mention at all of her heart. Why did Hillman say she was under treatment? And how could she question him without revealing that she'd seen the file? The situation put her in a bind.

It wasn't a case of him being a lousy record-keeper because the rest of the file appeared to be quite detailed and orderly. She considered a scenario where Dr. Hillman failed to diagnose Margaret's arrhythmia and was now trying to cover it up. But if that were the case, why would he bring it up at all?

Blanche got up to retrieve the pill bottle she'd taken from Margaret's medicine cabinet and had put in the vegetable bin of her refrigerator for safekeeping. She'd popped it into her basket without thinking much about it. Now she turned the bottle over in her hand and studied the label.

The prescription had been filled by Walgreen's Pharmacy at Villa Linda Mall on June 4 with the instruction: "Take

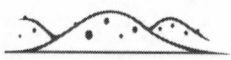

one a day, after eating." She remembered seeing it noted in Margaret's medical folder. Helen told her it was a common drug used to treat stomach ulcers which can result from taking too much ibuprofen over an extended period. They both knew that Margaret had taken ibuprofen daily to relieve her arthritis pain.

Now she opened the bottle and spilled a few capsules into her palm. The manufacturer's name appeared in tiny print on each capsule. She sniffed them. They had a vaguely familiar scent.

Blanche reflected on the fact that Margaret died less than two weeks after getting her new prescription. Could there be some connection? Could the prescription have been too strong, or have had some terrible side effect? Could it have brought on a heart attack? Could there be something *wrong* with the pills?

She'd ask Helen. Helen seemed to know about drugs.

But Helen sounded cautious on the telephone. "You. . . found. . .them?" she asked.

"I went into her apartment on Wednesday night, after the funeral, to look around," Blanche explained, trying to make it sound like a routine procedure. "I saw the pills and thought they might be important."

"Oh," was all Helen said.

"We saw the prescription for them in her folder, remember? Dr. Hillman wrote it just a couple of weeks ago."

"Oh." The reluctance in Helen's response was obvious.

"I thought it was odd that Margaret died so soon after seeing the doctor and starting on a new prescription. I thought there might be some connection—what do you think?"

"Well. . .I. . .maybe. . .," Helen said lamely.

"Look, Helen, don't worry, I'm not going to drag you into this any further. But you're the only one I can talk it over with right now."

"Well. . ."

"I'd like to have the pills analyzed," Blanche said, pressing ahead before Helen had a chance to object. "Do you know where I should take them?"

"Analyzed. . .?"

"Yes, you know, to make sure they *are* what the label says they are. Pharmacies make mistakes. So do doctors, even if they'd like us to think they never do."

"You could. . .try. . .the. . .State. . .Lab," Helen said.

"The State Medical Lab? Of course. Why didn't I think of that!" Then, shifting her voice to a more casual tone as though she had just remembered a minor detail, she said, "There's something else."

"Oh. . .?" Helen was on her guard.

"I found a curious list of names in a library book I picked up from Margaret's apartment the same night I found the pills. I planned to return it to the library, figuring Jack wouldn't know where it belonged. I think it was the book Margaret checked out last week. You mentioned she'd been in, remember?"

"Yes. . ."

"It looks like a list you'd make up if you were planning a party or something, only some of the people are dead, like Leland Strel and Peg Masterson."

Helen waited for her to continue.

"Then there's Lenore Richards—she's a friend of Margaret's from upstairs."

"Yes. . ."

"I think they used to bowl together for the Santa Fe High Rollers years ago.   Her apartment's just down the hall from Margaret's. But what about a Reginald Salazar—who's he?" Blanche was reading the names in order.

"Reggie. . .he's. . .a contractor. . .retired."

"He lives here?"

"Yes."

"Was he a friend of Margaret's?"

"I don't. . .know."

"What about Rose Armijo?"

"D. . .d. . .dead," Helen said.

"Recently?"

"About. . .six. . .months."

"What from? What did she die from?"

"Heart. . ."

"Did she live at La Mesa too?"

"Yes."

"Hmmmm." Blanche bit on her lower lip in concentration. "Sylvia Bell? Is she the widow of Regis Bell, the big cattle rancher?"

"That's. . .right. She's. . ." Helen stopped, unable to get the next word out. Blanche waited, knowing it would come. "Sick," Helen said finally.

"She's sick? How sick?"

"In. . .Health. . .Care."

"The Health Care Wing? How long has she been there?"

"Not. . .sure," Helen had trouble answering so many questions at once.

"Hmmm. . ." Blanche scribbled a note of her own next to Sylvia Bell's name. "Her name is underlined," she said.

"Under. . .lined?"

"Yeah, in pencil." She paused, gnawing on on her lower lip again. "Then there's the Rosenblums, Mary and Bud. I know them, saw them in the dining room the other evening. What about Adrian Curtis? Do you know him?"

"Died. . .last. . .winter," Helen said.

"Curtis died?"

"Yes," Helen confirmed.

"He has a check," Blanche said.

"Ch. . .check?"

"Yeah, a checkmark next to his name. I get it, the people who died are checked off the list—Strel, Masterson, Armijo, and Curtis. Margaret was keeping track."

"Odd."

"Very odd," Blanche said. "There're two more names I don't recognize, Merilee Jamison and Tomás Morales. Do you know them?"

"Morales. . .he's. . .new."

"Just moved here?"

"Few. . .few. . ." Again, Helen struggled for the right word while Blanche waited. "Months," she finished.

"What about Merilee Jamison?"

"Don't. . .know. . ."

"Maybe she doesn't live here. She has an `away' after her name, same as Rose Armijo."

"A. . .way?"

"Yeah, they've got little notations after their names, written by Margaret, I think."

"But. . .Rose. . ."

"Yeah, I know. She's not away, unless you're thinking in spiritual terms. She died. Was she away when it happened?"

"No. . .here."

"Hmmm." Blanche was biting her lip, thinking.

Helen was silent.

"Helen, I think this list is connected to whatever it was Margaret was going to tell me about last Monday," Blanche said, her voice rising. "Four of these people are dead, and three of them have 'NONE' written after their names."

"What. . .what. . .?"

"I don't know what it means," Blanche said. "Sylvia Ball has a 'NONE' after her name too, but she's not dead, not yet anyway. "But I'd be willing to bet that won't be the case for long, not according to the statistical evidence."

Blanche studied the list again and Helen waited again. "Reggie Salazar, Mary and Bud Rosenblum, and Lenore Richards have 'HERE' after their names. They *are* all here, that's true."

"T. . .True."

"And Mr. Morales has a question mark after his name. It's possible Margaret didn't know him." She sighed with frustration. "I know this list is important. Margaret was compiling it for some reason."

"Rose. . .Armijo," Helen said. "She. . .Adams." Helen paused, trying to find the right words.

Blanche could barely stop herself from trying to prompt her.

"Left. . .money."

"She left money to Adams? You mean in her will?"

"Y. . .yes."

"How much, do you know?"

"Three hundred. . . fifty. . .thousand."

"She left *three hundred and fifty thousand dollars* to Adams?"

"Yes," Helen confirmed.

"I wonder what he did with it."

Blanche continued staring at the list after she and Helen hung up. The names were written in a careful hand, like a schoolgirl's, on a plain white sheet of paper. It did not look like Margaret's writing. The notations, like some sort of secret code, were scribbled less carefully, in pencil. She was sure they'd been added by Margaret. Probably the underlining on Sylvia Ball's name too.

A glance at her watch told her it was quarter to eleven. She was still in her kimono and she'd told Esther that she'd be ready to leave for the Blue Portal at noon so they'd have time to eat and still get to the make-up demonstration at Dillard's by two o'clock.

Clearing off the table, she put the pill bottle back into the vegetable bin of her refrigerator and reassembled Margaret's records back into the green folder. She shouldn't leave all this stuff lying around where anyone could see it, she mumbled to herself. She glanced around the living room for a place to keep the folder safe. The desk, where she kept all important papers, was the logical choice. She yanked open the drawer and slide the folder in. But no sooner had she closed the drawer, she opened it again. The desk was too logical. She had a better idea and headed for her bedroom. Hoisting up a corner of her mattress, she slid the green folder in between the mattress and the inner spring. That was better. She gave a smart tug to the bedspread to smooth out a wrinkle.

Blanche was in the shower, feeling the hot spray loosening the muscles of her upper back when she got the next idea. They could skip the make-up demonstration. There'd

be another one in a month. She didn't think Esther would take much convincing, knowing how she felt about Reverend Adams. And she'd be the perfect accomplice.

* * *

"What will we tell him? That we were just passing by and decided to say hello?" Esther stopped dead in the middle of spreading chickpea paté with lingonberries, a specialty of the Blue Portal, on a piece of crusty French bread to stare at Blanche.

"Well, you know. We could say we were in the neighborhood and just thought of popping in. . ."

"Popping in?" Esther took a delicate bite of the French bread, being careful not to drop lingonberries on her pink linen shirtwaist which had a series of tiny, crisp tucks running across the top.

"Oh, Esther, it doesn't really matter what we say. I just want to have a look at the place and ask him a few questions."

"Fine with me," Esther said. "I've been curious about what's happening up there ever since Peggy died. But you do the talking. I'm just the chaperone."

* * *

"Ladies," Reverend Adams said in a kind of awkward surprise as he opened his front door to Blanche and Esther.

"Reverend Adams," Blanche said.

"To what do I owe this pleasure?" Adams stood with the door ajar but had not invited them inside. Blanche felt

like a door-to-door salesman politely being signaled to go away.

"Well, I thought we might visit a little," she said.

Esther nodded, smiling pleasantly.

"Visit?" Adams continued to stand with the door only partially open.

"Yes, if you'll let us in," Blanche said lightly.

"Oh, well, of course," he said, opening the door further so they could step onto the polished flagstone floor of the entrance. From there Blanche could see into the living room. The cool-looking white walls held several striking oil paintings in elaborate frames, and a large bronze sculpture rested in one corner.

"A lovely room," she said, stepping past Adams to get further inside. She was surprised by the elegance of the surroundings, the art and the handsome furnishings. Adams' twangy cowboy image seemed nowhere in evidence—he was even dressed differently from his usual Western garb, in a white linen shirt and cream-colored slacks.

"Are these paintings from the Masterson estate?" Blanche asked.

"I'm the trustee for them at the moment," he said stiffly.

"I see."

Blanche and Esther were fully in the room and looking more closely at the paintings. Blanche noted the fine wiring around them, which meant they were connected to an alarm system. They must be quite valuable, she thought. She inched her way over to the one which depicted a woman with an elongated face and neck.

"I hope we're not interrupting anything," she said to Adams over her shoulder. "We were up this way and remembered that you lived just off the Camino." Camino

was short for Camino del Monte Sol, one of Santa Fe's most picturesque streets running east off Canyon Road.

"Well, actually, I do have an appointment shortly," Adams said, looking at his watch.

"We won't be here long," Blanche said reassuringly. "This isn't a Modigliani, is it? I've never seen one in a private collection before."

"You know something about art, Mrs. Harriman?"

"A little," Blanche said. "May we sit for a minute?"

He gestured, helplessly, for them to go ahead. "Is there something in particular I could help you ladies with?" he asked. He continued to stand.

"Brancusi?" Esther asked in disbelief. She was gawking at the bronze sculpture.

"Yes," Adams said curtly. He shifted about in his cream-colored leather loafers, a departure from the cowboy boots he usually wore.

"How's the church coming?" Blanche asked. "We know that Peggy's generous gift"—here she gestured to encompass the room—"must have meant a great deal to you in getting things underway."

"You have an interest in my church, Mrs. Harriman?" Blanche knew by the way he asked that he was being sarcastic.

"Have you acquired the site yet?" she asked instead of answering his question.

"We have our eye on a site," he said, carefully measuring his words. "As I'm sure you ladies know, these things don't happen overnight."

"It wouldn't take long to sell a beautiful place like this," Blanche said innocently. "Have you listed it yet?"

Reverend Adams face turned red. "We're not quite in a position to sell yet, Mrs. Harriman."

"Oh?"

"Mrs. Harriman, really, I'm afraid it's not a good time to visit," Adams said, looking pointedly at his watch. "I have someone coming in just a few minutes."

"Of course," Blanche said, rising from the velvet settee. She decided to take a long shot. "One more thing, Reverend Adams. I understand you knew Rose Armijo?"

"Mrs. Armijo? Yes, I knew her." Adams answered in a clipped way.

"She must have thought highly of you."

"Mrs. Harriman, what are you getting at?"

"I didn't realize Mrs. Armijo was interested in your church too. With all the support you've had, I would have expected to see construction underway by now."

"Mrs. Harriman, I'm afraid the timing of my church construction is really not your business," Adams said. Now there was real anger in his voice. He began escorting them towards the door, sort of nudging them along.

Blanche pretended not to notice the affront. "How about Sylvia Bell? Do you know her too?" she asked pointedly.

Adams stopped and turned to Blanche. "I know you were a close friend of Mrs. Forbes," he said with intensity. "No doubt she shared some of her opinions with you. I just want you to know that she was not always right."

"I don't know what you're referring to, Reverend Adams," Blanche said, gliding smoothly past him to the door.

"I think you do, Mrs. Harriman," he said. "Margaret Forbes sometimes got involved with things that weren't really her business."

His tone suddenly struck her as menacing.

"She was a woman of high principle," Blanche said, an edge of anger in her own voice.

"She did not always have her facts straight."

Blanche raised an eyebrow.

"And facts and opinions are two different things," Adams said authoritatively.

"Kind of you to see us, Reverend," Blanche said, taking hold of the doorknob to let herself and Esther out. "I can see that you're a busy man."

She looked back at Adams, still standing in the doorway, as she and Esther walked down the flower-lined path to the drive where she'd parked her car. He hadn't uttered the usual niceties men of the cloth reserve for women visitors. He hadn't even said goodbye.

CHAPTER ELEVEN

"You're *loco!*" Nita spat.

The words rang through the thin wall separating Juanita's bedroom from the kitchen where her cousin, Nita, was arguing with Danny.

"Shut up or you'll wake her," Danny warned in a low voice.

"How could you even be thinking such a crazy idea? I can't believe you would do such a cruel thing."

"You won't think it's so cruel when you've got a million bucks in your hands."

"I want nothing to do with it," Nita said, her voice rising again. "It's not ours."

Juanita sat up in bed, barely breathing, listening closely.

"You're Juanita Gomez, just the same as she is," Danny said over the sound of the refrigerator being opened and shut. "If it weren't for you, she wouldn't be here at all."

"But what about Benito? You can't just forget him! If they send her back to Mexico, she's never going to be able to bring him here."

"That's her problem, ain't it?" Danny said. There was the sound of a can being popped open. "She should have thought about that before she used your papers."

The voices trailed off and Juanita could tell they had left the kitchen to go into the living room. She listened intently for a few more minutes but could pick up only muffled sounds.

Danny was scheming against her! He was trying to get his hands on her inheritance from Miss Forbes. What would he do? Turn her in to Immigration and send her back to Chihuahua?

Juanita's stomach muscles had constricted into a tight ball as she grasped the meaning of what she'd overheard.

She knew Danny had power over her cousin. He would work on her until she went along with his idea. They would say the money belonged to Nita. After all, she was the one who had the citizenship papers to prove who she was.

When Juanita first came up from Mexico to see about getting help for her son, it was her cousin Nita in Santa Fe who told her she could use her papers to get a job. No one would hire an undocumented Mexican, she said.

It made sense because they had the very same name. In Santa Fe, her cousin was called Nita, but the name given to her at birth was the same as hers, Juanita.

Remembering how she had been afraid and how Nita convinced her no one would ever find out, Juanita burst into uncontrollable tears and buried her face in the pillow to quiet the sounds. Poor Benito! If Danny turned her in, she'd never get to bring him to the U.S. for eye surgery! All these months away from him would have been for nothing.

It was too much.

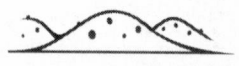

First the terror of crossing the border at Juarez, dressed in Bermuda shorts and an ugly pink polo shirt and carrying her cousin's driver's license. How frightened she had been that the border guards would ask her something in English and she would not be able to respond.

Then the humiliation of finding a job. Her cousin would help her fill out the application forms, but when it came to the personal interviews, Juanita would freeze. Even the little English she spoke seemed to fly out the window and she would burn with embarrassment.

"How long have you been in this country?" an interviewer asked her once, puzzled by the fact she didn't seem able to answer the simplest questions in English.

"*Veinte años,*" she had answered. Twenty years, because that's what her cousin's papers said.

The interviewer had shaken his head in disbelief and she saw an expression of disgust cross his face.

She finally got work in the housekeeping department at La Mesa, but it cost her a lot in terms of her pride. People would talk about her as though she were a piece of furniture or a subhuman species who couldn't understand the language of man.

But that was one of Juanita's secrets now. In the year she'd been in the U.S., she came to understand English quite well. She was too shy to speak it most of the time, but she didn't miss much.

Juanita got a tissue and blew her nose loudly, forgetting that she was supposed to be asleep. She'd said goodnight to her cousin at ten o'clock as she did every evening. Nita and Danny usually watched the late news on television and Juanita could hear it dimly from her bedroom before they went to bed.

But now she heard the door handle to her bedroom click and the door push softly open. She knew it was her cousin listening in the doorway.

"Juanita, are you all right?" Nita asked softly.

Juanita lay perfectly still and did not answer. Nita came over towards the bed, but Juanita did not move and kept her breathing even and her eyes tightly shut. Her cousin stood there for a minute before retreating. She drew the door shut softly behind her.

After that, despite straining to hear, Juanita could make out only the most muffled sounds for a short time and then the house fell silent. She lay awake for hours in the small, dark room, peering into the blackness as though some answer would reveal itself.

She was beginning to wish that Miss Forbes had never left her the money at all. At first, when the lawyer from the bank called and told her the amazing news that Miss Forbes had given her a million dollars in her will, she could not believe it. It was like a dream! She would only have to stay here a few more months before she could get the money and take it home. Then she could collect Benito and bring him to Santa Fe to have the clouds removed from his eyes.

She knew it was too good to be true. It was like some miracle too far away to reach and hold.

Only yesterday, she'd been frightened when Reverend Adams came up to her in the round meeting room off the lobby and said they must talk privately. The way his eyes stared at her made her feel anxious. He was not like the priests at home.

Adams started talking very simply to her, the way one talks to a young child. He spoke in English, but would toss in a few Spanish words here in there.

"Miss Forbes was your good *amigo*," he began.

Juanita had nodded politely, waiting for him to get to the point.

"You must have been *mucho* friends."

"She was very kind to me," Juanita said in Spanish.

"I know that she left you *mucho dinero*." Much money.

Juanita felt her face burning then.

"What will you do with all the *dinero*? A million dollars is a lot of money for a woman like you."

"*No se*," Juanita said. She said she didn't know what she would do with it. She thought rapidly. He was *un padre* and she should be able to confide in him about Benito and why she had to cross the border. But some instinct warned her to be careful.

"I want you to remember the Good Lord who brought you to such good fortune," Adams had said to her then, drawing himself up close to her face so that she could smell his sour breath, an odor she recognized as stomach turmoil rising up. "*Comprende?*"

"*Si*, Father," she said. Her eyes were large with fright and confusion.

"Give to the Lord, and the Lord will give to you," he said very pointedly.

"*Sí*, Father."

"I will be happy to receive your gift in the name of the Lord."

Juanita nodded.

"I will talk with you again, *comprende?*"

"*Sí*, Father."

Then Adams locked his eyes on hers meaningfully and left the room.

Juanita thought. So Reverend Adams had found out that she was going to inherit a million dollars from Miss Forbes and he wanted some of it. Probably for the church project he was always talking about, the one that made Miss Forbes so angry. She could give him some money, but not too much. She must first make sure Benito would be all right. If the Reverend tried to force her to give too much, she would pretend she didn't understand him.

Unless he knew about the false papers, of course. Then he could try to blackmail her. A wave of panic rose up inside her at that thought.

And now this terrible new problem. She could never in her wildest dreams imagine that Danny and Nita would try to cheat her like this. What if she went to jail! A shiver passed through her body.

But Danny and Nita would get into trouble too if they turned her in, she reasoned. They broke the law when they gave her the papers. They would have to face consequences too, and maybe they'd all go to jail.

Maybe Danny would turn everything around and claim that she *had stolen* her cousin's papers.

Maybe—the thought was so frightening that she tried to squash it back—maybe he would try to get rid of her in another way, a more permanent way, so that there would be just one Juanita Gomez to come forward and claim the million dollars. Juanita put her pillow over her mouth to stuff back the alarmed sounds coming up from her chest. She tried to steady herself by taking long, easy breaths and forcing her mind back to images of the sea which she had visited once as a child in Guaymas. It was her favorite escape exercise, one that had seen her through many a crisis.

She imagined bits of flotsam and jetsam floating and tumbling over wave after wave until out of sight.

Sometimes when she did this exercise, she could float the bits of rubble way out to sea and have an expanse of clear green water spread before her. That's when she would fall asleep. But tonight, as soon as she got one set of rubble cleared out, a new tumble of seaweed and debris would come pushing into the foreground. The ocean was churning and dirty, with menacing dark waters that refused to be quieted.

Finally, as gray dawn began to lift the blackness of night, Juanita drifted into a sleep wrought from exhaustion. Her last conscious thought, the one that allowed her to rest her fears for an hour or so, was that the time had come for her to confide in someone, someone who could understand how all this had happened. That person would have been Mrs. Forbes, but that was no longer possible. Now she thought she could trust Mrs. Harriman. She would talk to her in the morning and ask for help figuring out what to do. Without some kind of help, she knew she risked losing everything.

CHAPTER TWELVE

"What's this?" Lenore Richards, a brisk, athletic-looking woman in her mid-70's, adjusted her bifocals to read the list of names Blanche handed her.

"I found it in a library book I was returning for Margaret Forbes," Blanche said. "I thought maybe you could help me figure out what it means." She watched Lenore's quick eyes darting up and down over the names, trying, as she had, to identify a pattern.

"Me, Reggie, and the Rosenblums—we're all marked *here*," Lenore said, pursing her thin lips in concentration. "Merilee Jamison's marked *away*, but she's not away. I sat with her in the dining room last night."

"Is she the short lady with those little reading glasses halfway down her nose?"

"That's her. She must have them glued on."

"Was she close to Margaret?"

"I don't think they were terribly close," Lenore shrugged. "She moved here about six months ago, around the same

time you did. From someplace cold, Upper Michigan, I think."

"Has she been away recently?"

"Not that I know of. She didn't mention anything."

"What brought her to Santa Fe?"

"She has two sons, one back east and one in California. She wanted to live somewhere in between them, a place where the winters were mild." Lenore studied Blanche for a few seconds. "What's this about anyway? You sound like `The Chief Inspector.'"

Blanche snickered. "It's such an odd list, that's all" she said defensively. "It's as though Margaret was taking a poll or something. I thought you could help me figure it out."

Lenore weighed this. "You just found it?"

"Yes, in her library book."

"How do you know it belonged to her?"

"It's her handwriting." Blanche pointed to the pencilled notations.

"What about the names? Looks like somebody else wrote those."

"I don't know."

"Well," Lenore said thoughtfully, still staring at the list of names.

"Lenore, you knew her for a long time. Did she seem any different to you lately?"

"Different?"

"You know, like she was worried or unsettled about something?"

Lenore frowned. "I don't think so. I didn't talk with her all that much. We used to bowl together, but that was years ago. It was a real shock to hear she died."

"It was, wasn't it? I never knew anything was wrong

with her heart. We were planning to go to Mexico together next winter."

"She'd still have been on the bowling team if it weren't for that darned arthritis," Lenore said. She turned back to the list. "Maybe she was planning to throw a party and was trying to find out when everyone was going to be in town."

"But some of these people are dead."

"An old list?" Lenore made a skeptical face.

"What about Tomás Morales?" Blanche persisted. "Do you know him?"

"Nope." Lenore shook her head. "He must be new."

"It can't be an old list then."

"I guess not," Lenore said.

"How about Sylvia Bell? I understand she's in Health Care. Do you know what's wrong with her?"

"Something serious," Lenore said. "Cancer, I think."

"Adrian Curtis? Did you know him?" Helen had told Blanche that Adrian Curtis died last winter.

"I knew who he was, but that's about it. He kept to himself."

"Reggie Salazar?"

Lenore shook her head. "He doesn't spend much time around here. He's got a lot of family in Santa Fe."

"What do you think this `none' means after some of the names?"

Lenore shook her head again. "I don't know. There's four of them."

"I know," Blanche finished her thought out loud. "And three out of those four are dead."

* * *

Bud Rosenblum was tying the belt around a white terry robe as he opened the front door to his apartment. "Why hello!" he said, surprised to see Blanche.

"Forgive me for not calling first," she said. Obviously he wasn't expecting a Sunday morning visitor. "I just wanted to talk with you and Mary for a minute."

"Come in, come in." He ushered Blanche inside. The place looked like the reading room in the public library, with bookshelves lining three walls, and papers and magazines covering every surface. The Sunday *Times* was resting unopened on the hall table. Bud was a retired professor of political science from Columbia University.

"Who is it, dear?" Blanche could hear Mary calling from the direction of the bedroom.

"It's Blanche Harriman."

In a minute she was on her way into the living room, tightening her matching terry robe as she walked. "How nice to see you, Blanche. You'll have to excuse us—we tend to sleep in on Sunday mornings."

Blanche noted the high color in Mary's cheeks. "I'm sorry to interrupt, but I needed to see you both for a minute."

"What is it?" Now Mary had a look of concern. Bud moved closer to her.

"It's this list of names I found," Blanche said. She explained about finding the list in Margaret's library book and being curious as to what it could mean. "You know, she died so suddenly. I'm sure she left unfinished business."

The Rosenblums gave the list their full attention but they were as mystified as Lenore Richards had been. The only piece of information they could add was that Tomás Morales was a distinguished scholar of Latin American literature who had moved to Santa Fe this spring after retiring from Berkeley.

* * *

Blanche slipped the key to Margaret's apartment into the pocket of her yellow jogging suit. It was a little risky going in during the day, but it was a Sunday and she figured most people were at church or already enjoying brunch in the main dining room. Sunday brunch was the social highlight of the week for many La Mesa residents.

The idea had come to her as she left the Rosenblum's apartment. She wanted another look at the stuff on Margaret's desk. She had a feeling that there could be something that would shed light on the list of names. Maybe she'd open that manila envelope from Quenton & Co., find out more about Jack's dealings. No one would know it was she, and not Margaret, who'd opened it.

At Margaret's door, Blanche checked to make sure no one was in the hall. Then she let herself in, swiftly closing the heavy door behind her.

She noticed the smell of smoke as soon as she turned around. Then she heard a scraping noise, like a chair sliding back. Before she could absorb what it meant, a surprised-looking Jack Forbes came out of Margaret's study, holding a cigarette in his hand.

"Mrs. Harriman. . .what are you doing here?"

"Well, I, well. . ." She tried to think fast. "I had a key," she said, showing Jack the key which she still had in her hand. "Margaret borrowed a couple of books from me a few weeks ago and I thought I'd just try to retrieve them," she lied rapidly. "I hated to bother you with anything so trivial. Just thought I'd slip in here and find them and leave the key on the table when I left." Jack looked skeptical. "We exchanged keys, you see," she added.

"Exchanged keys?"

"I gave her mine, she gave me hers. In case we locked ourselves out. Of course Margaret wasn't prone to doing something like that, but I'm afraid I am." Blanche laughed nervously. "She had to come to my rescue a couple of times."

"Ah," Jack said.

"I should have called." She could see he was annoyed.

"The books are in here," he said, turning back into the study. She followed him and saw that he had been sorting the papers on Margaret's desk, tossing some into boxes on the floor and throwing many into an overflowing waste-paper basket. She saw what looked like the manila envelope from Quenton and Co. in one stack. Damn. She'd never get a look at it now. He gestured to the bookshelves. "What are you looking for?"

Blanche had to think fast again. "Two Hillerman mysteries," she said, spying a row of books by Tony Hillerman. "Ah, there they are." She grabbed two hardbound books off the shelf

"And the key?" he said, holding out his hand.

She handed the key to him. There was a funny look on his face, she thought.

"You know, I forgot all about having Margaret's key until this morning," she lied. "Then I thought I might as well save you some trouble."

"No trouble."

"If you need any help here. . ." She looked around at the disorder in the room.

"I think I can handle it." Jack paused and his tone shifted slightly. "Is there something in particular you're interested in, Mrs. Harriman?"

"Me?"

"Yeah."

"Oh, no, not really. Just the books." She tapped them lightly.

"Ah, the books."

"Well, I can see you're busy." Blanche took a step towards the door, then stopped and faced him again. "So what are your plans?" she asked.

Jack shrugged. "Haven't really thought about it."

"Will you be staying in Santa Fe?"

"Probably. It's home."

"Well, let me know if you need any help here," she offered again. "I could pack up the china or something."

"It's all under control," Jack said. He started walking out of the study, leading her towards the living room.

"Did you ever talk with Dr. Hillman again?" Blanche asked, a step behind him.

"Hillman? Why should I?" Jack turned around.

"Your aunt's supposed heart condition. I think it's so strange she never mentioned it."

Jack shrugged dismissively.

"Do you know about any special project she was working on recently?"

"Project? She always had some project," Jack said rather peevishly. He was standing near the front door, ready to open it.

"Did she ever say anything about a group of people here at La Mesa?" Blanche pulled the list of names out of her pocket. "I found this."

He looked at the piece of paper, frowning. Blanche watched his face carefully. "Means nothing to me," he said, handing it back to her.

"Do you know these people?" Blanche persisted.

"Couple of them. Masterson left that big estate on the East Side. Strel was an old friend of my aunt's."

"They're both dead now. So are Armijo and Curtis."

"How do you know it's my aunt's list?"

"I found . . .well, actually she left it at my place. I found it in a book I was borrowing from her." She was amazed at how easily the lie came.

Jack was looking at her curiously. "Can't help you out," he said in a way that closed off further discussion. He opened the apartment door for her.

"Well, then. . ." she put the paper back into her pocket and stepped into the hall.

"You should talk to Juanita Gomez," he said suddenly. "They were pretty cozy."

"Juanita?"

"Yeah, little Miss Juanita." There was something mean in the way he said it.

"You mean ask her about this list?"

"About who managed to score big-time by my aunt's death."

Blanche wrinkled her forehead, puzzled.

"Talk to her," Jack said as he began closing the door.

Blanche was in the elevator going downstairs, trying to figure out what Jack meant about Juanita. Idly, she flipped through the first pages of *Skinwalkers*, one of the Hillerman novels she took from Margaret's apartment. An inscription on the frontispiece caught her eye. "Here's a little background reading for your trip to the Reservation," it read. It was signed "Jack." With a sinking feeling in her stomach, she opened the second book, *A Thief of Time*. She thought she might already know the source of this one too. "Happy Birthday," it read, "from Jack."

* * *

It was time for brunch, so Blanche made a fast change out of her sweats and into the middy-bloused sailor suit she'd found on sale at the Junior Shop. With its plunging neckline and sassy gold trim, it wasn't a suit for little girls, she thought, noting the effect of a new French bra on her sagging bosom. She re-arranged her tousle of curls and examined herself in the full-length mirror on the back of her closet door. Not bad for seventy-eight.

Frank Zanders didn't think it was bad either, she could tell. He appraised her as soon as she walked in and motioned her over to the table for four where Esther and Ruby were already seated. They'd been watching for her.

"It is a rare privilege to be sole accompanist to such beauty," he said gallantly to the three of them. Margaret was right about Frank, Blanche thought, not for the first time. There was quite a charming spirit underneath that paunch and those thick glasses. She wondered if he'd ever tried contact lenses.

"What's good today, Frank?" Ruby asked, ignoring his compliment.

"Start with the fresh raspberries, almond cream sauce on the side," he said with exaggerated authority. "The raspberries will never be better. Melon you can eat all summer."

"Good advice," Ruby said. "And for the main dish?"

"That's a tough one today," Frank said, affecting a deliberately thoughtful expression. "Both the stuffed quail and the broiled trout are lovely. You may need to have some of each."

"Let's get going then," Ruby said, getting up. "Now that we have our game plan."

The elaborate Sunday brunch was served buffet style, with residents choosing the dishes they wanted as they went through the line. Frank, who was sitting to the right of Blanche, got up quickly and helped slide her chair away from the table. She saw his eyes sweep across her bosom.

"You're a hard person to track down these days," he said as they walked towards the first buffet table where elaborate, artfully arranged cornucopias of fruit spilled forth among fresh flowers. The adjacent table presented an array of delicate French pastries and hearty-looking nut breads along with various preserves and cheeses. After that, came the steaming hot entrees which were served by members of the dining room staff dressed in crisply starched pink uniforms.

When they had finished their salads and main courses and were enjoying the pears *flambé*, a famous La Mesa dessert dish, Blanche pulled out the list of names again. Ruby, Esther and Frank all puzzled over it, but none of them could explain it either. Frank was particularly determined

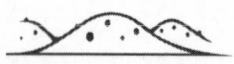

to crack it. He started to say something several times, to possibly draw some conclusion, only to check himself, frustrated.

"Let me work on this," he said. "Is this your only copy?"

It was, so he jotted down another copy for himself, writing on the back of a brunch menu.

"I think there's something here, but I can't quite put my finger on it," he said.

They were starting to leave the dining room when Bud Rosenblum waved, motioning Blanche over to his table.

"I'd like you to meet Tomás Morales," he said, introducing her to a silver-haired gentleman who was sitting with him and Mary. "I was just telling Tomás you found his name on that list."

Blanche showed Morales the paper with the list of names.

"I guess I'm the mystery man," he said, referring to the question mark after his name. "I'm here, if that's helpful. Afraid I can't be more enlightening than that."

Now she was down to just two names, Reggie Salazar and Merilee Jamison. Blanche had the feeling she wasn't going to learn much from either of them either.

* * *

Blanche was stretched out on her white couch, the sailor suit exchanged for the comfort of her hibiscus kimono. She'd called on Reggie Salazar and Merilee Jamison after brunch and found them both at home and willing to examine the list of names. However, neither knew what it meant. The only interesting thing was a small detail Mer-

ilee reported. She said that Margaret had called on her about three weeks ago and was asking her where her children and grandchildren lived.

"Where *do* they live?" Blanche asked.

"East Coast. Jim's in Boston with Caroline and their two kids, and Alan's in New York City."

Blanche sighed in frustration. She'd put in a full day's work, but where had it gotten her? She didn't really know any more than when she started.

She reached for her reading glasses and the *New Mexico Business Journal* that Frank had given her to read. It had Anthony Grace's picture on the cover. A round boyish face, not the face one would expect of a corporate "Man of the Year". The older she got, the younger they looked. Flipping through to the lead story, "Model on the Mesa: Retirement at its Best," she began to read about the 38-year-old graduate of Harvard Business School who was the toast of the town for managing the acclaimed retirement village, La Mesa del Sol.

It was a model for other retirement institutions being planned by the parent company, Esteem Enterprises. People from all around the country wanted to retire here, the article claimed, though Blanche knew that couldn't be attributed entirely to Anthony Grace. Santa Fe was pretty compelling all by itself and had been for about four hundred years.

She read that Grace had served an administrative internship with Children's Hospital in Boston, and then headed a health education project for the Navajo Health Authority in Window Rock, headquarters of the Navajo Nation. Interesting experience for a Boston boy, she thought. He also ran a federal health program for the elderly in Miami

Beach before joining Esteem Enterprises. He became administrator of La Mesa del Sol when it opened.

The rest of the piece talked about the special atmosphere of La Mesa, the changing perception of retirees, and the innovative programs Grace had initiated there. Blanche had read about them in a series of glossy pamphlets when she first moved in. Some things, like the Life Care Annuity Program, were out of her league since it required three or four hundred thousand dollars to enroll. It was appealing certainly, virtually assuring that a resident would be taken care of no matter how ill he or she might become. If she were in such a program, there'd be no need to worry about what Mitzi would do when she became too old and confused to make her own decisions.

Fortunately, the dismal prospect of such a situation still seemed a long way off, she thought as she closed her eyes and let the magazine come to rest on her chest.

CHAPTER THIRTEEN

"That's very kind of you, but I'm afraid I can't make it this evening," Avery Hillman said to the sophisticated-looking woman who had just invited him to join her group for a drink in the La Fonda's lounge after the concert.

Mrs. Williams looked acutely disappointed.

"But you're our Bach expert," she said coaxingly, looking up at him with azure eyes that matched her silk dress. They were in the midst of a crowd inching its way out of St. Francis Auditorium where the Santa Fe Chamber Group had just performed.

For a second, Hillman felt torn; it was so nice to be wanted. "I'm sorry," he said, wrinkling his forehead contritely. "I've got some work I have to get done at the office. We'll have to do it another time." He nodded to several others as he left the auditorium housed in the Museum of Fine Arts, just off the plaza.

Too bad to miss out on the little get-together, he thought as he walked across the street to the parking lot. Dr. Harris

and his wife would be there, and the Ortegas, Walt Wickers, Marjorie Beel. . . lots of important people. He liked being a part of their group.

Hillman had been in Santa Fe just two years, but he'd already established himself as a pillar of the arts community. One of the first things he did as resident physician at La Mesa del Sol was convince Anthony Grace that Esteem Enterprises should make a generous contribution to the world-famous Santa Fe Opera Company which was at the time facing a critical shortage of funds. Esteem Enterprises' magnanimous gesture had paid off handsomely all around. A number of influential Santa Feans who might not otherwise have paid much attention to the new retirement village on the hill, suddenly viewed it as a kindred spirit sort of place. La Mesa got the golden stamp of approval when Mr. and Mrs. Jason Colgrove III, longtime patrons of the Opera, sold their Hyde Park estate and moved in. Then and there, it become *the* prestigious address for a whole class of elite retirees, and concurrently, Avery Hillman was firmly installed as a member of the inner circle of Santa Fe society.

Missing one little gathering won't change that, he assured himself as he drove across town to La Mesa del Sol. In fact, Mrs. Williams was probably impressed by the dedication that inspired him to work on a Sunday evening.

* * *

J. J. Chavez was perched on a stool just inside La Mesa's front entrance, keeping vigil for residents who'd be returning after attending an event in town.

"Can't keep you away from the place, huh?" Chavez joked as he opened the door for Dr. Hillman.

"Yeah, got a little paper work to finish up before Monday comes around."

Hillman walked across the quiet front lobby and down the administrative corridor to his office suite. The scent of lemon polish rose to his nostrils as he unlocked the door and stepped into the reception area. He reached to his left for the light switch, then closed the door and turned with single-minded purpose towards his private office in the rear.

This shouldn't take long, he thought, loosening his tie and slipping out of his navy blazer before sitting down at his desk to slide open the center drawer. He'd figured out exactly how to handle the thing so as to allay any possible questions if they came up in the future. He reached for the dark green folder which he'd placed there on Friday. He shoved aside a few papers but didn't see it. Where was the dang thing? He plucked out a handful of papers to clear the drawer. What the. . .? He felt a knot forming in his chest. Margaret Forbes' file wasn't where he'd left it.

Hillman grabbed another stack of papers from a wire-mesh basket on the side of his desk and flipped through them. There were a couple of patient records needing completion, several lab reports requiring his signature, letters, invoices, various items requiring the attention of his secretary, Arlene. He knew he hadn't put the Forbes folder here, but he looked through the stack anyway. He'd deliberately set the folder aside on Friday so Arlene wouldn't transfer the patient information to her computer, which was the usual procedure when a patient died. He distinctly remembered pulling it out of the active file and putting it

in his top desk drawer after the Harriman woman was in asking questions.

He must have moved it somewhere else, he told himself, trying to suppress his anxiety as he began yanking open the other desk drawers. The top-right contained only his personal stationery and matching envelopes. In the middle were prescription pads and health brochures. The other drawers held forms, notebooks, drug promotions, a couple of old medical journals, business cards, notecards, and other office sundries. He shoved the contents of each drawer around, as though the green folder might emerge from the depths.

"Ridiculous," he muttered aloud, aware that his hands were trembling. "It has to be here somewhere."

Hillman pushed back his chair from the desk and went back to the front office. Maybe it was still in the file cabinet. He opened the top drawer and quickly flipped through the folders. . . Desmond. . . Estes. . . Feinstein. . . Fenn. . .Franklin. . . Gonzales.

No Forbes.

He went through them again, then slammed the drawer shut.

Hillman tried to think logically about where Arlene might have put the file if he'd left it out. He scanned her shining desk top, a cosmetic arrangement of a Chinese vase with silk flowers, large appointment calendar, and telephone. He tried to open the center drawer. Hell, it was locked. All of them were locked, he realized, as he tried each one.

Arlene was compulsive about filing things, he reminded himself. If he had left the folder out, she'd have found it and put it away somewhere. Maybe in one of her locked

drawers. He flipped through a stack of papers in a basket alongside her computer. Nothing.

Simple enough, he thought, reaching for the telephone. He'd just call Arlene at home and ask her. As he dialed for directory assistance, he glanced at his watch. It was quarter after ten. Don't be stupid, he told himself, slamming down the receiver as the operator answered. Arlene would think he was strange to be calling about Margaret Forbes' file at this hour on a Sunday night. He'd have to wait until morning.

He went back to his office and opened the top drawer again as though he expected the folder to materialize. He looked around the room. There must be something he was overlooking. It was probably right here in front of him and Arlene would go straight to it when she came in. He drummed his knuckles on the desk.

It was damned curious. He knew he'd pulled the folder from the file cabinet and put it in the top drawer. Now where the hell was it? Why didn't he take it home on Friday instead of leaving it here in the first place? Damn, he muttered aloud as he slapped the desktop in frustration.

Around ten-thirty, Hillman grabbed his navy blazer off the chair and turned off the lights. No use beating a dead horse. He'd just have to wait until morning.

* * *

Avery Hillman did not sleep well. He had a dream where a green file folder kept sliding off a stack of papers and he kept reaching for it. He could never get it to stay still. Every time he thought he'd put it safely down and turned his head, it began to slide off again.

Finally he awakened, his pajamas sticky with sweat. The luminous clock on the headboard read two-thirty. He flipped over the damp pillows and lay on his back, staring into the darkness of his bedroom.

After a while, he drifted off again but this time the dream that haunted him was an old and familiar one. He was back in medical school in Madison, Wisconsin in 1978. He and Carla were sailing on Lake Mendota and she was urging him to haul in the sails so the boat would heel. It tilted far over to one side, thrillingly close to the water. Then came the quick squall, a gale that blew up suddenly and capsized the boat, pouring them into the icy waters of the lake. Carla got caught underneath. The mast must have hit her head, the attending physician told him later.

Hillman sat up in bed, his heart thumping in his chest like a noisy compressor in an old engine. The nightmare was so vivid it could have all happened yesterday, and not for the first time he wished that he had died instead of Carla. He could still see her slim surgeon's hands just inches away, reaching for him under the water. If only he'd been able to grab them.

Hillman let his breath out in a loud gasp, the past and the present converging. He had to come up for air. He had to. His lungs were going to explode.

Now he threw off the covers and flung his legs over the edge of the bed, searching for his slippers. He'd learned it was better to get up and walk around when the night demons pursued him like this.

More than thirty years ago, when he was in his second year of medical school at the University of Wisconsin, he'd met Carla who was one year ahead of him. He'd been smitten by her dark beauty and pursued her shamelessly until,

flattered by his public courtship, she agreed to go sailing with him. Soon they were inseparable. They studied together, slept together, ate together, and on weekends, sailed on the lake together.

When she died, all the light went out from Avery Hillman's life. He stayed in his room the rest of the spring semester and took four incompletes. It was Mrs. Burns, the housemother, who forced him to re-enroll and resume his medical studies that summer. "Closing yourself off from the world isn't going to help what's inside," she'd said.

Hillman had never allowed himself to get close to another woman, although he was keenly aware he could have had his pick over the years.

Fully awake now, in the kitchen of his apartment, he poured a cup of hot water over a tea bag and watched the liquid darken and swirl. Carla would never believe it. He could hardly believe it himself. How had he gotten into such an amazing tangle? It wasn't as though he had planned it. It just seemed to have happened.

* * *

As he dressed for work on Monday morning, choosing a pale blue monogrammed shirt and light grey summer flannels, Avery Hillman tried to calm himself. It was important that he act as though everything were perfectly normal. There would be a perfectly reasonable explanation.

But why was he getting this odd feeling around the corners of his mind?

Hillman arrived at La Mesa del Sol before Arlene. He unlocked the door to the medical suite and let himself in, flicking on lights as he made his way to his office. Set-

ting down his briefcase, he checked his watch against the clock on his desk to verify the time. About ten minutes before nine. He couldn't resist flipping through the papers stacked in his basket, thinking that sometimes a lost item was right there in front of you all the time.

Who was he kidding? He'd gone through this stuff half a dozen times last night.

Arlene burst in, full of cheerful energy, about five minutes later.

"Nice weekend?" he forced himself to ask because that's how he'd greet her on any other Monday morning.

"Oh, didn't do anything special. Stayed home, soaked up a little sunshine, puttered around in my garden."

Hillman smiled. Arlene was an attractive divorcee, about forty-five, who was making herself very available to him, he knew. He could hardly believe she had sat around all weekend puttering in her garden.

"How 'bout you?" she asked.

"Oh, not much. Caught the last chamber music concert last night."

The look she gave him made him feel guilty, as though he should have asked her to go to the concert with him. That had occurred to him actually, but he'd decided against it.

"Listen, I seem to have misplaced the Forbes folder," he said as casually as he could. "Have you seen it?"

"Forbes? Did you look in the patient file?"

"It's not there."

"Hmmmm, I'll take a look."

She went back to her office and he could hear her opening and shutting file drawers. After a few minutes, she came back.

"That's funny. I don't see it either. Did you take it to make final notations?"

"You don't have it?" He was having trouble disguising the anxious tone in his voice.

"Well, I'll look again," she said. "But I don't see it."

"Well actually, I thought I had it here on my desk."

"You did take it then."

"I thought I did."

Arlene shot him a quizzical look as she leaned over the pile of folders and other papers on his desk, flipping through them one by one with long, red fingernails. Hillman sat still, watching her.

"Don't see it here either," she said, pouting prettily.

"I don't know what the hell happened to it."

"It has to be here somewhere," Arlene said. "I'll look around some more." She went back to the front office.

Hillman had three patients to see during the morning, two of whom he asked to meet back in his office after their examinations to discuss treatment. Each time, as he made notes on their charts while waiting for them to dress, he thought about the Forbes folder and whether Arlene had found it yet. At quarter to twelve, when the last patient left, he buzzed her on the intercom.

"Any luck on that Forbes folder?"

"No sir, I can't seem to find it anywhere." He could tell she'd looked hard for it because she sounded so disappointed. She said she didn't know where else to look.

There was a pause while Hillman thought.

"Dr. Hillman?" Arlene prompted.

"Yes, yes, I'm here. Just can't figure what happened to it, that's all."

"Well, I'll look some more after lunch. It's got to be around here somewhere. Do you want me to bring you something?"

"What?" He was distracted.

"A sandwich? Some yogurt? I could bring you something for lunch."

"Oh, no, thanks. That's all right. I'm fine."

Hillman sat at his desk, thinking hard, not moving. The anxiety he had managed to control earlier in the morning was overtaking him, and suspicion was curling in from a corner of his mind.

But how the hell could she have managed it?

He picked up the telephone and dialed a number.

"This is Avery," he said. "I think we'd better talk."

CHAPTER FOURTEEN

By five minutes after eight, Blanche had finished two cups of coffee. She allowed herself only two cups a day, and she tried to save one of them for lunch, but this morning she needed the extra caffeine to help her figure out what she would say to the State Medical Lab.

Most state government agencies were located in Santa Fe, the State Capital, but some important health and medical offices were attached to the University of New Mexico School of Medicine in Albuquerque, sixty-five miles to the south. Such was the case with the State Medical Lab. Blanche dialed the toll-free Albuquerque number listed in the directory.

"I'd like to have some pills analyzed," she told the woman who answered at the Lab.

"Yes, ma'am. What type of pills?"

"They're a prescription for Omeprazole," Blanche said. "But it's possible that something isn't quite right with them."

"Let me transfer you to Toxicology," the woman said. "Please hold."

Blanche waited through several rings until a man's voice answered.

"Toxicology, Larrison."

"I have some pills I'd like to have analyzed," Blanche said.

"Are you a pharmacist, ma'am?"

"No. I'd just like to have these pills analyzed."

"What sort of pills are they, ma'am?" Larson asked.

"Omeprazole, 40 milligrams," Blanche read off the bottle in her hand.

"Capsules?"

"Yes, little purple and white capsules."

"Prescribed locally?"

"In Santa Fe."

"You're taking them?"

"No, a friend of mine."

"I see," Larrison said. "And your friend wants them analyzed?"

"She's dead," Blanche said. "I want them analyzed."

"I see," Larrison said again. He paused. "So you want to verify the dosage, make sure they're OK?"

"Yes, I guess that's it," Blanche said.

"You think there's some connection between these pills and your friend's death." Larrison hadn't framed it as a question, but clearly he was grasping the reason for Blanche's request.

"There could be," she said. "That's why I'd like you to check them out."

"Who's the prescribing doc?"

"Avery Hillman. He's the physician-in-residence at La Mesa del Sol."

"La Mesa del Sol?"

"The retirement village in Santa Fe where I live, and where my friend lived."

"Have you asked Dr. Hillman about the pills?"

"Well, no, not exactly," Blanche said nervously. "I'd rather not."

"Uh-huh," Larrison said. "Well, you'll have to send them down. We'll have a report in two to three weeks."

"Two to three weeks?" She wanted to know something in two to three days.

"Yes, ma'am, two to three weeks. We got a back-log here."

"But I can't wait that long."

"Well, that's how long it'll take," Larrison said stubbornly.

"I need to know sooner," Blanche said.

"Well you can always take them to a private lab up there. It'll cost you, but they'll get on it faster then we can. We've got to take cases from all over the state, some of them come with court orders. They get priority."

"Can you recommend a lab?" Blanche asked.

"In Santa Fe? Hmmmm. . . let me see here," Larrison said. It took him a minute to come up with a name. "KG Labs up there is pretty good. They'll run a test in twenty-four hours if you're willing to pay the rush charges."

"KG Labs?"

"Right." Larrison gave her the telephone number. "It may cost you a couple hundred bucks."

"That much?," Blanche said.

"It'll be in that neighborhood."

She hung up the receiver and sighed. Was she being crazy about this? Unscrewing the top of the brown pill container, she looked inside at the cluster of capsules. There

was that sweetish smell she'd noticed before. She didn't
have a concrete reason for thinking something was wrong
with them; it was just one of those funny feelings. She bit
hard on her lower lip and picked up the telephone again.
There didn't have to be a reason. If she were wrong, well,
she'd be out a few hundred dollars, but at least she'd know.

"Dr. Harriman here," she said, in another of those sudden inspirations, when KG Labs answered.

"Yes, doctor, how may we help you?"

"I've got some Omeprazole capsules here," she said, trying to sound like she'd done this dozens of times before.
"Like to have them checked out as soon as possible."

"Checked out, doctor?"

"To make sure we have what we're supposed to have
here." Her voice had just a shade of gruffness.

"I see," the woman said. "Will you be sending the pills
over or should we have our driver pick them up?"

"Which is faster?" Blanche asked. Just then her door-chime sounded. It must be Juanita, who was due at nine
o'clock. "Just a minute, someone at the. . .someone on the
other line," she said, putting down the receiver. She scurried to let her in, telling her in a quiet voice that she was on
the telephone.

"Sorry, a patient calling—emergency situation," she
said as she picked the receiver up again.

"Our man makes collections between one and four this
afternoon," the KG Labs representative said. "Or you could
have someone drop them off this morning."

"I'll have someone drop them off," Blanche said, knowing the someone would be her.

"We'll finish up the paperwork when we get the pills.
Tell me your name again, doctor, and a number where you

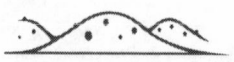

can be reached?"

"Dr. Blanche Harriman." She spelled her surname and gave her telephone number. "That's my private line."

"Were these pills prescribed for a patient of yours, Dr. Harriman?"

"Ah. . .yes," Blanche said.

"Was the prescription filled locally?"

"Walgreens at the mall," she said, reading from the label.

"Well, we'll get the tests started for you as soon as they come in. We should have something to report within forty-eight hours."

* * *

Juanita looked weary, with puffy half-moons the color of charcoal under her eyes. She was wearing white slacks and a loose-fitting pink smock with the words "La Mesa del Sol" embroidered over the La Mesa logo—a sunburst rising from behind a mesa.

"*Café?*" Blanche asked her.

"*Sí, gracias.*"

Blanche went into the kitchen to heat water. She used individual cone-shaped filters to brew the coffee one cup at a time, a slow but pleasing ritual which was deliberate enough to stop her from mindlessly drinking one cup after another. "You look like you could use a lift."

The kindly tone in Blanche's voice seemed to crack Juanita's carefully constructed composure.

"Oh, *Señora* Harriman." She suddenly burst into a heaving sob, sinking her face into her hands.

"*Pobrecita*, what is it? What's wrong?" Blanche put

down the hot kettle and went to Juanita, stroking her back as one might comfort a small child. Juanita's sobs turned into little hiccup-like breaths as she struggled for control. Finally she took a deeper breath and squared her shoulders, pulling away slightly from Blanche's hand.

"Come, sit down," Blanche said. "Let me get you a tissue." Blanche ushered her into a kitchen chair and set a box of tissues before her. "What's wrong?"

Juanita just stood there shaking her head from side to side and sniffling into the tissue.

"Tell me, dear, what is it?

* * *

All Blanche knew about Juanita was that she was from Mexico and spoke mostly in Spanish. She'd been recommended by Margaret, and that was like being recommended by the Dean of Yale Law School or maybe the President. Margaret was demanding. If she was pleased with Juanita's performance, no further recommendation was necessary.

"How long have you been in the United States?" Blanche asked.

"*Por uno año.*" For one year.

"Is your family here?"

"*No, estaban en Mexico.*" They are in Mexico.

"Do you have children?" Blanche watched as Juanita nervously twisted a gold wedding band around her ring finger.

"*Si, un hijo.*" One son.

"They're with their father?

Juanita did not meet Blanche's eye. "They have no father," she said in Spanish. "He went away a long time ago."

She spread the fingers on her left hand, emphasizing the wedding band. "This is nothing."

Blanche nodded, grateful that her textbook Spanish could keep up with Juanita's delivery.

"My son, Benito, has a sickness and that is why I came to the United States to earn money to help him." The words came in a burst, as though they had been waiting to rush out.

"What's wrong with him?" Blanche asked.

"He is almost blind. When I was pregnant with him, there was a disease of measles in our town. He was born with only a little sight."

"Maternal rubella?"

"*Sí*, that is what it is called."

Blanche knew of other cases. Babies could be born with serious vision impairments, sometimes blindness, as a result of the mother's exposure to German measles during pregnancy. "What do the doctors say?"

"An operation could help him, but it takes much money," Juanita said. She took a deep breath and blew her nose.

"So you came to work here?" Blanche feared she'd break down again, she looked so miserable.

"*Sí*."

"You have your visa?" Thousands of Mexicans carried U.S.-issued visas which allowed them to live and work in the States.

"No." The admission brought a new rush of tears from Juanita. She buried her face in her hands.

"Come now, dear, it's not the end of the world," Blanche said, trying to comfort her. She knew that many Mexican citizens worked in the Southwest illegally, living in constant fear of being discovered by the Immigration and Nat-

uralization Service. "I know a good lawyer, Estevan Ortiz. He'll be able to help. After all, these are special circumstances. I'm sure the authorities will be understanding."

But Juanita was shaking her head. There was more. "I have been using my cousin's papers," she said in Spanish. "Her name is the same, Juanita Gomez, and she is legal."

"She's a citizen?"

Juanita nodded.

"Does she live in Santa Fe?"

"*Sí.*"

Blanche took a moment to consider the impact of this revelation. "Well, that makes things more complicated," she said, "but I'm sure we can get Mr. Ortiz to help." Actually, she did not feel as confident as she tried to sound. "Your cousin, the other Juanita Gomez, did she give you permission to use her papers?"

"Yes, but. . ." Juanita hesitated, took another deep breath, and blurted out the rest of it. "But now she wants to get rid of me."

"Get rid of you?"

"Her husband—he wants to get rid of me," Juanita corrected. She withdrew a fat envelope from her large woven handbag and handed it to Blanche. Her hand was shaking.

Blanche took the envelope which bore the return address of Holmes, Holmes, and Wedbury, Attorneys at Law. She unfolded the wad of papers and read the title on the top sheet: "The Last Will and Testament of Margaret Branson Forbes". A feeling of mild alarm rose up in her chest. How had Juanita gotten hold of Margaret's will?

She read rapidly through the first page, a standard declaration of Margaret's being of sound mind, and a statement that this will, dated April 2, superseded any previous

wills. The next page began listing the beneficiaries to her estate. "To my nephew, Jack Lyndon Forbes of Santa Fe, the corpus of my estate, minus the delineated gifts which follow, to be held in trust until he attains the age of sixty-five." A complicated explanation of the trust provisions took up several more pages. The bottom line was that, according to the terms of the trust, Jack would receive two thousand dollars a month until he turned sixty-five.

That was about thirty years from now! It would be infuriating to Jack, Blanche knew. Two thousand a month was barely enough to survive on, especially with the cost of living in Santa Fe. It certainly wouldn't support the lavish lifestyle he was accustomed to.

Blanche's eyes flitted down through the paragraphs. Three-million dollar trust established for the Santa Fe Children's Museum, of which Margaret had been a founding member. A million each to UNICEF, Oxfam, and CARE, three international children's organizations which Margaret had long supported. To the Special Arts Project of Santa Fe, a half-million; children's collection at the Santa Fe Public Library, a half-million.

Frank Zanders was right—there were a lot of millions.

Near the bottom of page six, she finally made the connection: "To Juanita Gomez of Chihuahua, Mexico, currently residing in Santa Fe, one million dollars."

"For you?" Blanche asked, surprised.

"Yes, it is for me," Juanita said. "But now my cousin and her husband see an opportunity to steal it from me. If I am not here, they can collect the money for themselves."

"But that's absurd! You *are* here."

"I heard them talking. They are planning something." Juanita was on the verge of tears again.

"What are they planning? To turn you in to the Immigration authorities?"

"That's what it sounded like at first, but now. . ." Juanita stopped, not daring to say the rest.

"Now?" Blanche prompted.

"Now I think they are planning to kill me!"

"Oh come now, child. This is not the movies."

"*Es verdad*," Juanita insisted passionately. "It's true. I heard them talking."

Blanche saw the frantic look in Juanita's eyes. "Then we'll have to move fast," she said, taking command of the situation. "If what you say is true, we have no time to lose." She stood up, ready for action. "I'll call Estevan Ortiz," she said, reaching for the telephone.

Juanita's eyes looked glazed, spent of their energy.

"Tell me," Blanche asked as she was dialing, "did Miss Forbes know about all this? That you were working here without proper documentation?"

"I don't know," Juanita said. "But she said to make sure my papers were in order."

"When did she tell you this?"

"About two months ago, when I told her about Benito."

Just about the time Margaret was revising her will. Blanche couldn't suppress a fleeting smile. Margaret must have suspected that Juanita was in the U.S. illegally. She left her a million dollars, knowing she wouldn't be able to claim it until she cleared up her Immigration status.

* * *

Blanche called the lawyer, Estevan Ortiz, and he'd agreed to see them at 1:30 that afternoon. The next problem was

finding Juanita a safe place to stay because she was too frightened to return to her cousin's house. Blanche decided to try Ruby whom she knew had two bedrooms.

"It's a complicated family thing," she told her. "She lives with her cousin, but she needs to get away from the house for a couple of days."

"How long?" Ruby asked.

"Oh, just a few days. She won't be any trouble. I'd keep her here, but it's the first place they'd look because she works for me."

"I'm not going to get into any trouble over this, am I?" Ruby asked suspiciously.

"Ruby, would I do that to you? The poor girl just needs a few days to rest where no one will bother her."

"All right, bring her over."

Then Blanche called La Mesa's personnel office, saying she was Juanita's aunt, and reported that she wouldn't be able to come to work the rest of the week. "Nasty virus, terrible cough, and she's running a fever," she said.

She was stumped briefly on what to do with the car Juanita used to drive to work. It belonged to Danny, and he'd come looking for it if she didn't bring it home tonight.

"Follow me downtown and we'll leave your car in the La Fonda garage when we're done at Ortiz' office," she told Juanita. "No one will pay attention to a car parked there for a couple of days."

* * *

Estevan Ortiz was solemn. He sat erectly, his thin, elegant hands crossed neatly on the desk across from Blanche and

Juanita. "Do you understand that you face immediate deportation?" he asked Juanita in Spanish.

"*Sí.*" She nodded somberly.

"However, because of the extenuating circumstances, I will try to secure a temporary permit if Mrs. Harriman is willing to sponsor you."

As Ortiz drew out the facts of Juanita's predicament, Blanche looked around the handsome office which was housed in a 100-year-old adobe constructed when New Mexico was still a Territory. Three striking Indian pots rested on a shelf over his desk, two with the lustrous black shine characteristic of Santo Domingo and Santa Clara pottery, and the third, from Acoma, was painted in a black and white geometric design. A handsome Two Grey Hills Navajo rug hung over a curved *banco*, and next to it, a diploma granting Ortiz a degree in jurisprudence from Georgetown University Law School.

Suddenly a chord struck in Blanche's memory. Not the booming kind, just a tingling little one. She'd seen the usual assortment of degrees hanging in Dr. Hillman's office too, and he also had a Navajo rug, an unusual one. It had a caduceus woven into it and the initials "N.H.A." at the bottom. That stood for Navajo Health Authority. She just remembered reading in the *New Mexico Business Journal* that Anthony Grace had worked for the Navajo Health Authority too.

"Mrs. Harriman?" It was Ortiz, interrupting her thoughts. "Are you willing to sponsor Mrs. Gomez as a visitor?"

"Yes, certainly."

"You must complete the forms and bring them to me by nine o'clock Wednesday morning." He was assembling a sheaf of papers into a folder for Juanita to take with her.

"I must warn you that Immigration is not inclined to look favorably on the falsification of documents," he added to Juanita. "This cousin of yours also faces federal charges if we prove she was a collaborator."

Juanita looked very nervous.

"The biggest worry right now is keeping Juanita safe," Blanche interjected. "We'll have to worry about the federal charges later."

"Unfortunately the law has been broken, Mrs. Harriman," Ortiz said sternly. "I'm afraid we have a number of things to worry about here, and it will serve everyone best if we don't lose track of any of them."

CHAPTER FIFTEEN

They left Danny's car, a beat-up maroon sedan, in La Fonda Hotel's parking garage.

"It'll be fine there for a few days, don't worry," Blanche said as Juanita got into the Cadillac to go back to La Mesa with her. "We could call the police with an anonymous tip that a maroon sedan's been abandoned there."

Blanche had one more errand before returning to La Mesa. Juanita waited in the car while she stopped at KG Labs, located near the hospital on St. Michael's Drive, to drop off the Omeprazole capsules. "Larrison is expecting this," she said in an official tone as she patted the brown envelope containing the pills. "ASAP."

"And you are?" the receptionist at the front desk inquired.

"Prescribing doctor," Blanche said. "It's all in the package." Then she turned abruptly to leave, stopping just before the exit to repeat her order: "ASAP".

"You better lie down before you fall over," Ruby said to Juanita when she and Blanche finally arrived at her apart-

ment. Juanita's eyes were dark and puffy from crying and lack of sleep. "Your room is all ready. Come." She put her arm around Juanita's shoulders and steered her towards the guest bedroom.

"Poor thing's a mess," Ruby said as she returned to the living room. "What's this all about anyway?"

"It's pretty complicated," Blanche said. She gave Ruby an abbreviated version, ending with Juanita's fear that Nita and Danny might kill her over the inheritance from Margaret Forbes.

"That's a pretty generous bequest to leave your cleaning lady," Ruby said bluntly. "Do you think there's anything fishy about it?"

"Fishy?"

"Yeah, fishy. Do you think it's on the level?"

"Of course it's on the level," Blanche said. "One look at that girl and you know she's in real pain about all this."

"No pain, no gain," Ruby said, making a silly grin which Blanche ignored. "How'd you get in the middle of it all?"

"She was going to pieces right in front of me. I had to help her."

Ruby's voice grew serious. "Do you think she could have had anything to do with Margaret's death?"

"I know you could put together a theory about Margaret being murdered for a million dollars, but I don't think Juanita's capable of anything like that," Blanche said. "She's not a devious person."

Ruby raised an eyebrow. "She's a little devious or she wouldn't have gotten herself into this bind with the Immigration authorities."

"That's different," Blanche said in her defense. "She was desperate about her son. And besides, she wasn't even ex-

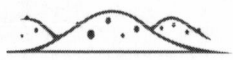

pecting to be named in Margaret's will. She told me she wished she hadn't been because it's just messed everything up."

Ruby raised an eyebrow. "Do you think this cousin and Danny could have been involved?"

"I don't know," Blanche thought aloud.

"Do you know these people?"

"No, and I can't say I have any desire to."

"What happened to that list of names you were showing around over the weekend? Have you figured what that's all about?"

"No," Blanche shook her head

"You'd better watch who you're talking to, by the way."

"What do you mean?"

"I was castigated by his highness, Mr. Grace, this morning."

"What for?"

"'Interfering with a state inspection' was, I believe, the way he phrased it."

"Come on, get serious."

"I am serious. He called me said there'd been a complaint from Rasmasson about my being over in Health Care during the inspection last week. He said he'd appreciate my not interfering in the future."

"Touchy," Blanche said in an exaggerated way. "What'd you do? Trip him?"

Ruby laughed. "I just ruffled his feathers."

"Well, I'm much more discreet," Blanche said smugly.

"Yeah, you're discreetly going around La Mesa questioning how Margaret Forbes died," Ruby huffed. "I'm just

telling you to watch your step. They don't like anything unpleasant around here."

* * *

Blanche could not quite place the smell, but there was something naggingly familiar about it. She smelled it as soon as she unlocked her apartment door. Spicy, like some woodsy-scented furniture polish, only no one had been here to polish the furniture. She ran her finger across the top of the coffee table, leaving a little trail between the fine particles of dust. She was walking towards the bathroom when she remembered. It was like the aftershave that Arthur used. She inhaled deeply, trying to hold the scent and the memories it invoked. Where had it come from?

A frown furrowed her forehead and she got a funny feeling in the pit of her stomach. Had someone been in here? The maintenance office always called first if they were going to send a person in while she was away. Could they have forgotten to call? She went to the telephone and dialed building maintenance.

"This is Blanche Harriman in Apartment 127. Did you have someone in here this afternoon?"

"Are you having a problem?"

"Not that I know of," Blanche said. "But I think one of your staff people may have been inside my apartment."

"Let me check the log."

Blanche waited.

"I don't show anything on your wing today. I know they've been changing filters on a lot of air conditioners. Do you want us to send someone over?"

"No, thanks," Blanche said, hanging up. Already the scent was eluding her. Maybe she'd imagined it. It had been a long day and her head was pounding. She needed two aspirin and a nap.

She opened the medicine chest and reached for the aspirin bottle which she kept on the top shelf, upper right hand corner, next to the antacid tablets. But for some reason, it wasn't in the usual place. It was down on the left, by the vitamins.

It was a small thing, but she felt a mild irritation. She liked to keep things in a certain order so she'd know exactly where they were when she needed them.

* * *

Blanche had settled into a welcome nap when the ringing of the telephone awakened her. It was almost four-thirty.

"I've got an offer you can't refuse," Frank Zanders said.

"Try me," she said, shaking off her grogginess.

"Enchiladas, home-made, at my place. Seven o'clock."

"You're right, I can't refuse." Blanche was fully awake now, checking the time on her watch. She had time to shower, fix her hair, and change. The black-and-white caftan would be perfect, and she'd been itching for an occasion to wear it. Sophisticated, but with a touch of. . .wild zebra. Exactly what a mature female should wear to a mature male's apartment for a casual dinner.

Frank was amazing. He had a pitcher of Margaritas waiting on the coffee table when she arrived. He poured her one in a frosted glass and offered her guacamole and chips before excusing himself to pop the chicken enchiladas into the oven. "They just need to heat through—

enough to make the cheese melt," he said. Her mouth watered at the tantalizing aromas coming from the direction of the kitchen—roasted chili, garlic, cumin, cilantro. The man was talented!

"Mmmmmm," she said, happily dipping a blue corn chip into the guacamole. "How'd you learn to do all this?"

"Bachelorhood," Frank said. "It forces one to come to grips with the mysteries of the kitchen."

"It hasn't put that kind of pressure on me, I'm afraid. My specialty is Le Gourmet, found in only the most exclusive frozen food departments."

Frank laughed. "You're a modern woman."

The way he said `modern woman' made the heat rise to her cheeks. Maybe it was the Margarita; these weren't the virgin variety and she'd better pace herself.

"How long have you been a bachelor?"

"It's been eight years since Barbara died. And as you can see, I've not been fading away." Frank patted his substantial paunch.

"Do you exercise?"

"Oh, I make a stab at it, try to swim a couple times a week. Do you swim? Not that you need the exercise, of course." Frank's eyes swept admiringly over the zebra stripes.

She wondered how she'd look in a swimming suit. It had been a while since she risked that sort of exposure. "I try to get to T'ai Chi twice a week," she said. "Once in a while I take an early walk at the mall."

"Hey, it's time," Frank suddenly announced, looking at his watch. "Let's get it on the table."

He removed the steaming enchiladas from the oven. Plump chunks of chicken and generous mounds of grated

cheese were layered between soft corn tortillas and smoth-
ered in the divine-smelling green chili sauce. Then, as
Blanche watched, impressed, he garnished each plate with
lettuce and tomatoes and a dollop of sour cream.

It wasn't exactly a diet dinner, but who could worry
about a diet at a time like this? She'd think about dieting
next week, before trying on swimming suits.

As they sat down at the small dining table, Frank lighted candles and poured them each a glass of Saint-Emilion,
French, 2009, she noted.

"My compliments to the chef," Blanche said, raising her
glass in a toast.

"And to a most gracious guest." Frank touched the lip
of his wine glass to hers, making a little ping.

"You should enter the chili cook-off down in Albuquerque," Blanche said appreciatively between mouthfuls.

"Ah, you're flattering me."

"Well I may be flattering you, but I'm serious. You
could win, hands down."

"I'd need you to handle the publicity."

"I charge, you know, but I'm worth it."

"Ha!" Frank's belly shook with laughter. "I'm sure you
are." He wiped the corners of his mouth with his napkin.

Blanche felt herself blush. It had sounded more sugges-
tive than she meant. The wine must be going to her head.

"I get the feeling there's no stopping you once you start
on something," he said, steering the conversation in a different direction. "How's the Forbes case coming along?"

"I'm waiting on a report."

"Report?"

"Oh, you know, technical stuff," she said, waving her
hand and ignoring the puzzled look on his face. She'd re-

solved to keep it to herself about taking Margaret's pills to KG Labs, particularly since Ruby warned her for talking too much. And she had the feeling if Frank knew, he'd start to worry about what she was doing.

"You know, that list of names you showed me?" Frank said. "I see a common denominator in that everybody on there, at least the ones I know, are pretty well-heeled."

"You mean *very* wealthy?"

"Yes, big money."

"The only one I know much about is Peg Masterson. She left a fancy house up on the Camino, worth over a million, I'm sure."

"She did," Frank said. "And I know she had a Life-Care annuity here."

"Life Care?" Blanche's fork was poised midair with enchilada on it. "Grace's program?"

"Right. It takes $300,000 to $400,000 up front, so you've got to be pretty financially comfortable to get into it."

"How does it work?" Blanche remembered reading about it in the slick brochures La Mesa distributed, but she didn't bother with the details since it was beyond her means.

"It's sort of like buying health insurance, only it's more comprehensive. Your initial investment depends on your age and physical condition. Once you're enrolled, La Mesa takes care of you for as long as you live, no matter how sick you get. Everything's covered, your apartment expenses, private nursing, all the medical costs after Medicare quits paying."

"Surgery?"

"Everything. Hospital, doctors, the works. And if you

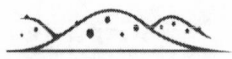

have a serious illness that drags on, they take care of you here in the Health Care unit."

"Some people can be sick for years and years."

"That's right. It's a gamble. La Mesa can lose money if a person is sick for a really long time." Frank was mopping up the chili sauce from his plate with a hot tortilla, and Blanche couldn't resist doing the same even though she was about to burst. "On the other hand, La Mesa makes money if it goes the other way."

"They probably use those actuarial tables to figure out the life expectancies," Blanche said.

Frank looked surprised by her having this sort of knowledge.

"Arthur," she reminded him, "was in the insurance business."

"Oh, right." Frank sat back and took a sip of wine.

"How about the others on that list. Do you know if anyone else is enrolled in this Life-Care program?"

Frank pursed his lips, thinking. "I think the Rosenblums have signed up. Lenore Richards may have too—you could ask her. And Leland Strel might have been another one. He had the money, and it would have been logical for him to enroll in a thing like that because he didn't have any family to look after him if he got really sick."

* * *

Frank walked Blanche down the hall to her door just before ten. She resisted the urge to invite him in for a nightcap. She had too much on her mind tonight.

"It's been a lovely evening," she said as she put her key into the doorknob. She slipped her hand inside to flick on

a wall switch which lighted the lamp on the entrance table, but she remained standing in the doorway. She faced Frank.

"I've enjoyed it immensely myself," he said, his eyes crinkling up behind his thick lenses as he smiled.

"You're a hard act to follow," she said. "But I'll see what I can do with Le Gourmet and a salad."

"Sounds terrific." He leaned down and brushed her cheek with a kiss. It seemed very natural. "Get a good night's rest."

"Thanks, I need it."

"Next time—after you're rested up, I won't let you off so easily, you know."

"I know," Blanche said, grinning. She stepped into her apartment and waved good-night before closing the door.

* * *

Blanche was in bed under her fluffy comforter with her eyes closed, but she wasn't asleep. She was thinking about Arthur. She imagined she could still smell his spicy cologne, and that at any minute he'd come out of the bathroom and slip into bed next to her in his striped pajamas.

It was silly, of course. Sometimes when she was very tired, she allowed herself to have the harmless fantasy that Arthur was still by her side. It helped ease her into a dreamy sleep.

But it wasn't working tonight. The more she thought about Arthur, the more alone she began to feel. She listened intently to the silence of her room. She thought about the spicy scent in the apartment this afternoon.

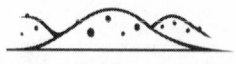

Someone could have come in, but how would they have gotten in and what had they wanted?

She knew the nurse on duty always had a pass key to be able to respond to emergency call buttons. Maintenance could get in day or night in the event of a fire, broken pipes, something like that. Juanita had a key, of course.

Blanche suddenly became aware of her own heartbeat which seemed to intrude on the silence. Where was the spare key that Margaret had kept for her? She'd returned Margaret's key, but hadn't thought to ask Jack for her own back. If he came across it, he might not know it belonged to her. Or then again, he might.

Blanche shivered, feeling exposed and vulnerable. She was tempted to call Frank, but dismissed the idea. She didn't know him quite that well yet. After another restless twenty minutes, she turned on the bedside light and picked up one of the Hillerman novels and her reading glasses. But she only made it through two paragraphs before her mind began to wander. Finally she got out of bed and grabbed her robe.

Padding out to the kitchen in her slippers, she opened the refrigerator and checked the contents of the vegetable bin. The list of names was still there, alongside a black velvet pouch containing her pearls and her good earrings, and the obituary notices for Peggy Masterson and Leland Strel. There also was a mesh bag of wrinkled-looking carrots and some very limp celery.

She took out Leland Strel's obituary and read it closely. Frank said he was a likely candidate for Life-Care because he didn't have any family around to look after him. That appeared accurate; the story didn't make a single reference to family members. She read through Peggy Masterson's

obit again and was struck by the fact that no family members were mentioned for her either. She pulled the list of names out from under the celery. Peggy and Leland both had a "none" after their names. It was possible. . .

Then she returned to her bedroom and slipped her hand under the mattress. The Forbes folder was still there and a quick glance at its contents assured her it hadn't been touched. She slid the folder in deeper, between the mattress and innerspring.

The last thing she did before going back to bed was what enabled her, finally, to sink into a few hours of sleep. She dragged a kitchen chair to the front door and by tipping it an an angle, hooked the top rung of its ladder back underneath the doorknob. It wasn't a strong barrier, but it would present unexpected resistance if someone tried to enter during the night. Then she got out an armful of cooking pots and lids and piled them precariously on the chair. If anything or anyone disturbed their delicate balance, they'd come crashing down and sound one heck of an alarm.

CHAPTER SIXTEEN

The knocking seemed to be coming from far away. Knock, knock, knock, knock. Blanche forced one eye open to see the clock without lifting her head from the pillow. It wasn't quite seven-thirty and someone was pounding on her front door. Groaning, she pushed herself out of bed and groped for her kimono, thrusting her arms into it as she stumbled out of the bedroom.

At the door, she encountered the stack of kitchen pots which she'd stacked strategically the night before. "Just a minute," she called as she unhooked the ladder back chair from the door knob and sent a couple of them clanging to the floor. She looked through the peephole and found herself staring at the red, pockmarked face of a man she'd never seen before. On his head was a dirty baseball cap and stretched across his prominent belly, an olive-drab T-shirt that said "And Proud of It" in block letters.

"Who is it?" she called through the locked door.

"I'm lookin' for Juanita Gomez."

"Juanita Gomez?" Hearing Juanita's name was like re-

ceiving a sharp wake-up call. She knew immediately who it was.

"Yeah, I'm a relative of hers."

It had to be her cousin's husband. Blanche had thought about the possibility of him coming around looking for Juanita. She unlocked the deadbolt and cracked the door open a few inches.

"I'm trying to find her," he said, peering in at Blanche. "She didn't come home last night."

"She didn't come home?" Blanche said, looking as genuinely puzzled as she could.

"She never showed up."

"Are you. . .?"

"Her and my wife are cousins," he said. "She lives with us."

"She was here yesterday," Blanche said, clutching her kimono and trying to keep her voice calm. She could see part of a complicated tattoo on one muscular arm.

"Yesterday, huh?"

"Yes, in the morning."

"What time?"

"Maybe you'd better tell me your name," she said.

"Gomez, same as hers. Dan Gomez."

"Well, Mr. Gomez, she was here yesterday at her usual time. She came in around nine-thirty and stayed until lunchtime."

"You ain't seen her since then?"

"Actually, I had to leave before she was done," Blanche said, ignoring the challenge in his tone. "So I last saw her sometime during the morning." It thrilled her to lie so coolly.

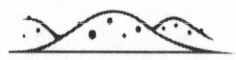

Gomez was looking into the room through the partially open door.

"I've been conducting an experiment," she said, tracking his eyes as he took in the pots on the floor.

But he didn't seem to care. "She say anything about being sick?"

"Sick?" Blanche hadn't prepared for what now struck her as an obvious line of inquiry. "Well, now that you mention it," she said thoughtfully. "I thought she looked a little. . ."

"Downstairs they said she called in sick," Gomez interrupted. He wasn't interested in Blanche's comments. "But that's a crock."

"My goodness." Blanche looked as perplexed as she could.

"She said her doctor wouldn't let her come to work," Danny said. "But that's bullshit 'cause she ain't got no doctor."

"Oh dear," Blanche said.

"Who else does she work for around here?"

"Look, Mr. Gomez, I'm afraid I can't tell you anything more. And I don't appreciate your waking me up at such an early hour." She cinched her robe tighter.

Danny caught his lower lip under his front teeth and narrowed his eyes. "You better be leveling with me," he said.

"I beg your pardon?" He looked like a ferret, she thought.

"You heard me. If you're hiding something, there's gonna be trouble."

"Are you threatening me?"

"You're damned right I am," he said. His dark eyes flared like they had yellow flames behind them.

"I think that's about enough," Blanche said crisply, her hand on the doorknob.

Gomez jammed a boot into the door frame. "When you see her, you tell her to get her hide home," he said, nearly spitting the words in Blanche's face. Then he turned and stomped off down the hall.

* * *

Blanche's hand was trembling as she bolted the door after Gomez. She could understand Juanita's fear. Dan Gomez was a real creep, and she had no doubt of the physical strength behind the angry face.

"Keep Juanita out of sight," she told Ruby from the telephone in her bedroom. "Don't let her out of your apartment."

"Don't worry. We're not going anywhere. I slipped a Valium into her tea last night, so she's still asleep, and I'm not fit to be seen by anyone at this hour of the morning."

"Good work," Blanche said. "I could have used one myself last night.

"You'll come by later?" Ruby asked. "It's sort of hard for me to talk with her."

Blanche laughed. She'd forgotten Ruby's Spanish was more elementary than her own.

"Listen, she understands more than you think. Just tell her Danny Gomez is looking for her and that she's not to leave your apartment for any reason. I'll come by later on."

"OK."

"You can help her fill out those forms for Ortiz. He's going to need them first thing in the morning."

* * *

Lenore Richards reminded Blanche of a large pear, about six feet tall with small breasts and wide hips. She was on the La Mesa swim team and Frank said she took it seriously, practicing laps in the pool nearly every morning. Whenever Blanche saw her, she was on her way somewhere—the pool, the Plaza, a play, or about to drive to Albuquerque for some event. She gave the impression of always being in a hurry, never having quite enough time for everything she had to do.

"I'm researching an article about family relationships," Blanche had told her on the telephone. "I wonder if I might stop by and ask you a few questions. It won't take long."

"I didn't know you were a writer."

"Well, I'm trying," Blanche said. "It's a story about how people living in retirement communities relate to their families on the outside." Blanche had decided to heed Ruby's warning and not advertise her real mission.

"What do you want to know?" Lenore asked when Blanche arrived and was sitting across from her in her living room.

"Have you ever been married?" Blanche poised her pencil over a notepad, prepared to jot down Lenore's answers. She could see her swimming suit straps showing outside her green terry shift and knew that Lenore was ready for her workout in the pool.

"Only for about forty years," Lenore grinned. "My husband's been dead for seven."

"Children?"

"Two daughters, both married. One's here and the other's in Denver. Both non-producers. No grandchildren." Lenore clipped out the information as though it were a timed interview.

"Do you see them often?"

"I see Cassy—she's here in Santa Fe—two or three times a week. Sometimes she comes over here, or we meet downtown for lunch. I always go to their place for dinner on Sundays."

"You get along well then?"

Lenore looked at her oddly. "Yes, with Cassy and her husband anyway. I don't see Donna and George all that much."

"They're in Denver."

Lenore nodded. "They have their own lives, both working full time. I can't really expect them to get down here a lot."

"Of course."

"Where's this going to appear?" Lenore glanced at her watch.

"Oh, *Psychology Today* or *Modern Maturity*, I'm not sure."

"Really?" She sounded impressed.

"Well, I'm going to try."

"Why not," Lenore said. "Listen, would you mind walking down to the pool with me? I don't have much time."

"Do the Rosenblums have children here?" Blanche asked as they stepped into the hallway.

"They have a daughter in Albuquerque. She teaches at the University," Lenore said, pressing the elevator button.

"And they have a son who's a chef. He's at L'Epicure, the new restaurant up in Tesuque, about five miles from here."

"So they see each other often?"

"All the time."

"What about Reggie Salazar?" Blanche asked. "You know him, don't you?"

"Oh sure, everyone knows Reggie. His family's been in Santa Fe for generations. He has a couple of grown kids and a bunch of grandchildren. They visit him all the time."

"It's nice to have family close by as you get older, I guess," Blanche said as the elevator doors closed behind them. Personally though, she wasn't convinced. She was thinking how glad she was that Mitzi didn't live in Santa Fe.

"In case something happens," Lenore agreed.

"Are you enrolled in La Mesa's Life-Care Plan?" Blanche asked as they stepped out on the first floor and walked towards the pool area.

"Yes, I am. As you say, it's nice to have family near by, but it's also nice to know that you're never going to put a strain on them financially if something does happen. Having Life Care takes care of all that."

"One last question," Blanche said. "Did you know Rose Armijo? She died last year."

"I knew her a little. She tended to keep to herself."

"Family?"

"Not in Santa Fe. She had a couple of children, but they live somewhere else." Lenore was fidgeting with her bag, antsy to get going into the dressing room.

"Thanks so much," Blanche said. "You've been really helpful."

Lenore had the door open. "Don't forget to give me a credit," she said as she waved good-bye.

* * *

"Mother!" A familiar voice rang out as Blanche walked across the front lobby heading for her apartment. She whirled around.

"Mitzi! What are you doing here?" *Oh, no, of all times for Mitzi to show up!*

"Just thought I'd surprise you," Mitzi said, arms outstretched. She was obviously pleased with herself.

"Well, how. . .how nice," Blanche managed as she embraced her.

"You look great." Mitzi stepped back to take in Blanche's coral jumpsuit and concho belt, her gaze ultimately resting on the top of her head. "You've got a new hairdo."

"Why, yes, I do," Blanche said, running her fingers through the tousle of red curls.

"Quite a color."

"You like it?"

Mitzi shrugged noncommittally.

Blanche appraised her daughter's neatly cropped brown hair which hadn't changed noticeably since high school. She was wearing a blue chambray shirtwaist straight out of another era. Mitzi never took a chance with contemporary fashions. In fact, Mitzi rarely took a chance with anything. "What are you doing here?"

"Seeing you! I got in about an hour ago and checked into the El Dorado. I was going to call, but I thought I'd surprise you."

"Well surprise me you did," Blanche said, her heart fluttering. Mitzi didn't tend to act spontaneously so she couldn't help but wonder what was behind this unexpected visit.

"How long can you stay?"

"A week!"

"Really!" Oh God, she hated surprises, and the timing of this one couldn't have been worse.

"So, where's your apartment?" Mitzi was bursting with enthusiasm.

Blanche pictured the pots she'd left in the entry in her hurry to get to Lenore Richard's. Mitzi would never understand. "The cleaning lady's there this morning," she said. "You'll have to wait." She couldn't believe she was fibbing to her own daughter. "Let's get some lunch in the dining room. I don't have a scrap of food in my place anyway, and I'm starving."

"Right now?"

"Sure, you can see my apartment later." She steered Mitzi in the direction of the dining room, ignoring her hesitation at making an on-the-spot decision on something so important as lunch. "You'll see how well we eat around here."

Blanche recommended the salad bar, knowing there'd be chilled prawns, and curried chicken salad, and fresh fruit cups. Within minutes they had their plates abundantly filled and were sitting at her favorite table overlooking the garden.

"Nice place," Mitzi had to admit.

"I told you."

"I know it's been a hard time for you though."

"Mitzi, who have you been talking to?"

Mitzi's face turned red. In a way, Blanche hated to do this to her, but she'd suspected that Mitzi had come to Santa Fe for a reason. She also knew she could make her spill it.

"Christine Wilson called me."

"Christine called you?"

"She said you were acting a little weird."

"What do you mean, weird?"

"Having trouble accepting Margaret's death."

"I knew you're weren't totally on a pleasure jaunt."

"Oh, Mom."

"Oh, never mind," Blanche said. "I'm glad you're here." She felt genuine affection for her daughter, but couldn't resist a mild reproof. "But you should have given me a little notice. I've got an appointment this afternoon and I'm afraid it's too late to change it."

Mitzi looked chagrined.

"But let's have an early dinner tonight, just the two of us," Blanche said. "I'll make a reservation at the Coyote Cafe and pick you up about six."

* * *

Le Boutique Fleur operated a flower stall in a corner of the book shop just off La Mesa's front lobby. The flowers were fresh, beautiful, and expensive. Blanche surveyed the possibilities and then put together an extravagant bouquet of exotic spotted lilies, long-stemmed fuchsia roses, and elegant greens to set it off.

"Must be a special occasion," the owner said admiringly as he arranged the flowers with greenery and bundled them in hot pink tissue paper.

"It is." Seventy-two dollars worth in fact, she noted as she signed the charge slip. She hoped it'd be worth it.

Bouquet in hand, Blanche walked toward the Health Care Wing. As soon as she stepped through the double doors, she was struck by the different atmosphere in this

part of La Mesa del Sol despite the obvious efforts to make it look cheery and colorful. In fact, the determination to be upbeat made it all the sadder, she decided. She knew the layout of the wing, four pastel corridors spreading out from a circular nursing station like spokes from a wheel. (The base of the nursing station had been painted to resemble a pot of flowers with green-striped stems rising to a mural of pink and orange blossoms just under the counter.) There were ten rooms down each corridor, smallish rooms uniform in design and furnishings: a bed, bedside tray, two chairs. They left little opportunity for individual expression.

Blanche had learned Sylvia Bell's room number, C-3, by calling La Mesa'a front desk and pretending to confirm a flower delivery. If she stopped at the nurses' station to ask about Sylvia, she'd draw attention to herself and have to register as a visitor. It would not be a wise move, she decided. Her plan was to walk right by the station with the huge bouquet shielding her face.

"Wait a minute, where are you going with that?" A nurse looked up from her charts as Blanche was half-way past.

"Delivery," Blanche called over her shoulder.

"You can leave it here, at the desk," the nurse called after her. Blanche pretended not to hear and kept walking briskly ahead towards the "C" corridor which was pale green and veered off to the upper right. The nurse apparently decided it wasn't worth pursuing and turned back to her charts.

C-3 was the second room on the left. Blanche felt a mixture of excitement and dread as she approached, having no idea what she might find.

Sylvia Bell was small and fragile, with a long single braid of grey hair hair pulled back from a sweet face. She was sitting up in bed, a little bird feeding herself from an assortment of small bowls on a tray.

"From a special admirer," Blanche announced brightly, coming into the room with the big bouquet.

Sylvia looked up, a puzzled expression on her face.

"Just thought you might need some cheering up," Blanche said, coming close to her. "I'm Blanche Harriman. I live over in residential."

Sylvia smiled a bit tentatively.

"How are you feeling?"

Sylvia shrugged her thin shoulders and shook her head. Not good.

"How long have you been here?"

"A month. More than a month," she corrected.

"What's wrong exactly?" Blanche was looking around for something to put the flowers in, but she didn't see a vase anywhere. She should have thought of that.

Again Sylvia shrugged. "High blood pressure. The doctor's afraid I'll have a stroke."

"Dr. Hillman?"

"Yes."

Blanche was examining the contents of the little bowls on Sylvia's tray. Cottage cheese, fruit, soup, jello. They'd hardly been touched. "Special diet?"

Sylvia grimaced.

"Deliveries are usually left at the station," a voice interrupted. It was the nurse who'd been at the station when Blanche walked by. She looked at Blanche, then at the flowers, and softened. "Have you got something to put them in?"

"I didn't bring a vase," Blanche said.

"I'll get you one from up front," she said. "But I'm afraid I'm going to have to ask you to say goodbye when I come back. Sylvia needs a lot of rest. She's under strict orders."

"I just need a few minutes," Blanche said. "I have a message from an old friend."

The nurse left and Blanche stood very close to Sylvia who was looking quite confused.

"I'm the old friend, only I'm a new friend who happens to be old, so it's not really a lie," she said, her voice lowered confidentially.

Sylvia gawked at her.

"Oh never mind. I came here because I wanted to ask you a couple of quick questions."

Sylvia furrowed her forehead, trying to make sense of this visit.

"I'm writing an article," Blanche began. "It's called 'Relating to the Outside World'. . ."

CHAPTER SEVENTEEN

Blanche backed the Cadillac out of its slot and began weaving her way through La Mesa's underground garage, her tires making high-pitched squeals on the polished asphalt. She paused at the exit and pressed the remote control button on her dashboard to lift the garage door. In seconds she was leaving the premises on La Mesa Drive. A sharp left connected to Chavez Road which ran straight downhill until it intersected St. Francis Drive, known locally as the Taos Highway.

Because Chavez Road banked steeply, Blanche automatically applied her right foot to the brake pedal to slow the behemoth Caddy's downward momentum. Oddly, the brakes didn't seem to take hold. She pressed again, but the pedal just wobbled loosely and had no effect. The big car was picking up downhill speed while Blanche slammed the pedal to the floor again and again, her own senses sharpened to a screaming pitch. It was useless. The car was beginning to race down the sharp incline. Looking ahead, wildly, she caught a glimpse of three cars lined up at the

intersection with the Taos Highway, waiting for the light to change.

Sweat broke out on her temples as she continued slamming the brake pedal to the floor, but nothing stopped the car's unrelenting forward motion. In a flash of inspiration, she grabbed the handle of the parking brake and yanked it up. It slowed the motion for an instant but then the force of two-and-a-half tons of rolling steel overcame the minor constraint of the parking brake like an elephant brushing off a fly.

The big Fleetwood pounded down the hill.

From some deep recess of memory, she recalled a mountain-driving lesson Arthur had given her forty years ago. She shoved the gear-shift lever into low, putting extra drag on the engine. She felt hopeful for a second as the car slowed, but it wasn't enough. She was still rolling dangerously fast. Panic swelled in her chest. She grabbed the ignition key, about to turn off the engine, then immediately changed her mind. That would lock the steering.

The car ahead was so close she could read the license plate. It was only seconds before she would ram it, propelling it and the cars in front of it into four lanes of highway traffic.

Then suddenly, without stopping to formulate the plan, blind adrenaline took over and she yanked the steering wheel sharply to the right. The Caddy's front wheels plunged into a culvert off the side of the road, bringing the vehicle to a halt amid a great reverberating crash of steel and rock. Blanche's head slammed against the windshield, cracking it into a giant spiderweb, before she was thrown aside like a giant rag doll.

CHAPTER EIGHTEEN

Blanche sensed an odd thing happening. Her bed was jiggling, and she felt like she was moving along a track. It was like being in a sleeping compartment on the train. There was a shrill sound. . .a siren? Was she dreaming?

She opened her eyes slowly, cautiously, and looked up to see a shiny white ceiling with a red cross painted on it. A medical emergency. There'd been a medical emergency. Then she became aware of the straps across her chest. It was her. She was having a medical emergency. She was in an ambulance.

"What. . .what happened?" She shifted her eyes to her left where she perceived the closest human presence. It was a young woman with freckles and light hair, in a neatly pressed blue shirt. When the woman leaned over her, Blanche could read her name tag: Norma Sanchez, Emergency Medical Technician.

Then Blanche noticed the cords running from her chest. She was hooked up to something.

"Your heartbeat is being monitored," Norma said, following her gaze. "You've been in an accident."

Ah, she remembered now. She'd been driving down the hill from La Mesa and couldn't stop. The brakes wouldn't work. "What happened?" she asked groggily.

"You were coming towards St. Francis Drive when your car went off the road. The impact threw your head against the window."

"Am I hurt?" Blanche raised her hand to her head, anticipating how warm, sticky blood would feel. Instead she felt a soft bandage.

"A cut. Doesn't look too bad. I think you're going to be all right."

Blanche closed her eyes. Her head was pounding.

"What's your name?" Norma asked.

Blanche didn't feel like talking.

"Come on now, don't go to sleep on us." Norma squeezed her arm lightly. "We're almost there. Tell me your name, please."

Blanche told her, but didn't open her eyes.

"Address?"

"La Mesa."

"Up there on the hill?"

"Yes." Oh God, her head was pounding something awful.

"We're pulling into the hospital emergency room now. No sense going to sleep now. They'll just wake you up again."

Blanche opened her eyes. Suddenly she felt cold. She shivered.

"It'll be just a minute now," Norma said, drawing a blanket up around her.

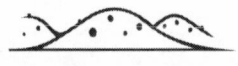

Blanche could hear the ambulance doors being opened. Another attendant, a young man also in blue, wheeled her cot out of the vehicle and into the emergency room to a little cubicle surrounded by white curtains. Vaguely she registered a doctor who didn't look old enough to be a doctor, examining her head. He peered earnestly into her eyes, examining her pupils, and asked her the same questions Norma had. When he held a steely cold stethoscope to her chest, she was swept with a wave of nausea and motioned urgently, not trusting herself to open her mouth to speak. Luckily, an assisting nurse saw what was happening and thrust a large pan in front of her at the critical moment.

She vomited until her head felt like it was going to crack in half and then she broke out in a cold, clammy sweat. The nurse wrapped a pre-warmed blanket around her but even then it took several minutes for the shivers to subside and by that time the doctor had disappeared into another cubicle.

"I think you've had a slight concussion," the nurse said. "Your body is feeling a little shock. We'll give you something to help the nausea and the pain, but first I need to ask you a few more questions."

"OK," Blanche mumbled. She felt awful.

"How old are you, Mrs.. . . Harriman?" She stopped to look at a sheet of paper attached to a clipboard.

"Seventy-eight." No sense fibbing under the circumstances.

"So you're on Medicare," the nurse said, making a note. "Do you have a supplement?" Another insurance policy to supplement the fees covered by Medicare.

"A.A.R.P." American Association of Retired Persons.

"Is there someone we can call, some family member, to come down to the hospital?"

Mitzi! Oh my gosh, she'd forgotten about Mitzi. "What time is it?!"

"Time? It's about quarter to seven," the nurse said.

"My daughter's at the El Dorado."

"Hotel El Dorado?"

"Yes, downtown, the El Dorado." Blanche's head was splitting.

"Does she work there?"

"No, no. Visiting." She wished the nurse would stop asking her so many questions.

"We'll call her for you. What's her name?"

"Mitzi."

"Mitzi Harriman?"

"No, no. Dyer." Dyer was her married name.

The nurse was squeezing something tight around her right arm. Ah, she was taking her blood pressure. "One fifty-eight over ninety," she said.

The emergency doctor returned to unwrap the bandage which the EMTs had put around Blanche's head. He separated her hair and poked around a very tender spot. It hurt.

"Looks like there could be a little glass in here," he said to the nurse. "Let's clean it out, and then we'll take a few stitches."

Blanche thought she was going to be sick again, but the nurse put a steadying hand on her arm and handed her a small cup of liquid medicine. "Here, drink this. It'll help control the nausea, and the headache too."

"We'll keep you here until your daughter arrives," the

doctor said. "Then we'll see how you're doing." He patted her on the shoulder and was gone.

A technician, a man of about forty-five with a neatly-trimmed beard, came in shortly after the doctor left. "I'm going to give you a new hairdo here," he said cheerfully. "It shouldn't hurt—I'm putting a little something on your scalp to numb it."

It took Blanche a few seconds to realize he was going to shave off her hair around the wound. Involuntarily, she raised a hand to protect herself.

"I'll do it as stylishly as I can," the technician said, gently lowering Blanche's arm. "It'll hardly show under these beautiful curls—trust me."

He dabbed disinfectant into the cut and then gently began to pry around with a pair of long medical tweezers. "Don't need this in your head," he said as he removed a thin sliver of glass and showed it to Blanche. "That's the worst of it. A couple of stitches will close this up nicely. You're lucky."

The cut was closed with eleven sutures. Blanche was instructed not to wash her hair for a week, or she would risk re-opening the wound.

"A week!"

"Seven days from today," the technician repeated. He made another notation on her chart, snapped it closed, and patted her arm as he left.

"Mom, oh my God." Mitzi came into the room just as the nurse was wrapping a long strip of fresh gauze round and round Blanche's head.

"I'm all right—it's just my head." Blanche pointed to the bandage. "I could pass for a Civil War veteran, don't

you think?" She spoke lightly, trying to provide reassurance to Mitzi who looked like she was about to faint.

"Is it serious?"

"Ghastly headache."

"Is she going to be all right?" Mitzi directed the question to the nurse.

"She'll be fine."

"Oh, Mom, how did it happen?"

"I was on my way to town to pick you up. The brakes went out coming down the hill."

"You couldn't stop?" Mitzi's eyes got big.

"Impossible. I steered the car off the road so I wouldn't crash into the three cars ahead of me at the highway."

"You. . .you went off the road?"

"It seemed like the right thing to do at the time. Now I'm not so sure."

"What does the doctor say about your head?" Mitzi gestured to the bandage.

"A minor concussion. He said I'll be fine in a day or two."

"I think you should stay in the hospital, at least overnight," Mitzi said.

Blanche started to shake her head in protest but it hurt too much and the effort made her start to feel nauseous again. She knew she couldn't argue with Mitzi right now; she didn't have the strength.

"You've had a concussion," Mitzi went on, as though Blanche wasn't the one who'd just told her that fact. "You've had stitches, and you look as pale as a ghost. There's no way you're going back to your apartment until we're sure you're going to be all right."

The emergency room doctor, whom Mitzi managed to track down in the hallway between two other patients, said it was their decision. He'd approve a 24-hour admission given the patient's age and general condition.

Now what exactly did that mean? That she was over the hill? Blanche glared at Mitzi, but kept her mouth shut.

* * *

Around eight-thirty that evening, Blanche was eating chicken noodle soup and fruit salad in her hospital room while Mitzi looked on. "Sure you don't want some?" she asked.

"No thanks, really. I'll get a bite at the hotel."

"It's not bad." Blanche's headache was better and she felt hungry—a good sign. She'd even gotten some color back in her cheeks and she'd been able to fix her hair, rearranging the curls so they partly disguised the white bandage. The doctor had come up to take a look at her before leaving the hospital for the evening and signed a provisional discharge for the morning, the provision being that all would go well for Blanche during the night.

"Visiting hours are over," Mitzi said just before nine. "I'd better let you get some rest."

"Don't worry about me. It's just a cut."

"Mother," Mitzi said in her just-barely-tolerating-it tone. "You had a concussion."

"How's the car?" Blanche suddenly remembered the car.

"The police towed it away. They said the front end is pretty bad. We're supposed to have someone take a look at it and see if it can be fixed."

"It *has* to be fixed," Blanche said anxiously. "I'll call Dick Masters in the morning." Masters was Blanche's mechanic, recommended to her by Margaret when she moved to Santa Fe.

"Don't worry about it tonight," Mitzi said.

"You'd better get some rest yourself," Blanche said. "You're the one who looks pale now."

"See you in the morning then," Mitzi said, kissing her lightly on the forehead.

* * *

The ten o'clock TV news drowned out most of the hospital sounds although periodically Blanche could hear a ping-ping from a patient call button. It reminded her of a sound she used to hear at Dayton's Department Store in Minneapolis. She watched the screen lazily as a meteorologist pointed out low-pressure zones on the state map. Then suddenly, the voice of the KOAT newscaster snapped her back to attention:

"This bulletin just in. . .

"Dr. Avery Hillman, medical director of the nationally-known La Mesa del Sol Retirement Village in Santa Fe, died this evening as the car he was driving went out of control on State Highway 30 between Los Alamos and Santa Fe. Dr. Hillman, fifty-three, was returning to Santa Fe after attending a meeting of the State Medical Society in Los Alamos. Witnesses at the scene said the car, a late model white Mercedes, left the road at Dead Man's Curve and went down a sixty-foot-deep ravine, flipping several times before bursting into flames."

Blanche froze, barely trusting that she'd heard it right. A shiver ran through her body and for a minute she barely breathed.

Avery Hillman, dead. Right now, his body could be here, at this very hospital.

What a coincidence, she and Avery Hillman, both having accidents on the same night.

Ping-ping. A call button was sounding in the corridor. The KOAT news team was saying good-night.

All of a sudden it hit Blanche like a bolt of lightning. It was stupid of her not to have realized it sooner.

Her brakes were intended to fail coming down La Mesa hill, and she was not expected to get off with a mild concussion either. She was expected to be in the same condition as Avery Hillman.

That meant she wasn't safe now. Especially alone in this room.

She hesitated only a second. Then she reached for the telephone on the side of her bed and dialed La Mesa del Sol. She asked the receptionist to connect her with Frank Zanders.

CHAPTER NINETEEN

The telephone startled Frank. He'd been propped up in bed reading *Financial World* and must have dozed off. "Blanche?" he said. "Where are you? I can barely hear you."

"Frank, listen, I'm in the hospital and I can't talk long."

"In the hospital?" His voice rose in concern.

"Don't worry, I'm fine. I'll explain everything later. In the meantime, I need to ask a tremendous favor. I need you to help get me out of here. Tonight."

"Tonight? You want to leave the hospital tonight?"

"You've got to trust me on this, Frank." She kept her voice low so the staff wouldn't overhear her as she told him about her accident, and then about Avery Hillman's accident. "I think they were both planned, and whoever planned them is going to be disappointed that I've come through so well."

"You think you're in danger?" Frank sounded worried, but a little skeptical at the same time.

"I *know* I'm in danger," Blanche said with the firmness of a Congressional proclamation. "Especially if I stay here."

"But they won't let you walk out the door at midnight," he argued.

"I need a disguise."

"A disguise?"

"Yes, a disguise."

"What kind of disguise?"

"Something official—something to make me look like a doctor."

"A white coat?"

"No, no. Some golf slacks, a tennis sweater, something like that."

"Golf? Tennis?" Clearly he wasn't tracking her request very well.

"You know, something that a doctor might be wearing if he were on call."

"You want men's clothing?" Frank didn't sound very sure about this plan.

"That would be good."

"Ah, OK," Frank responded uncertainly.

"It doesn't need to be anything special—just some casual stuff." Blanche said. "I don't have anything here. Mitzi took my clothes to have them cleaned. She was going to bring me a change in the morning."

"I see."

"Frank, please," she urged. "A pair of old trousers and a shirt—oh, and some shoes."

"Shoes?"

"Yes, shoes. Doctors wear shoes."

"But mine are way too big for you."

"Maybe some sneakers. Don't worry about it. All I have to do is walk out of the hospital."

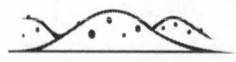

Blanche described the layout of the medical floor in relation to her room which was about fifty feet west of the nurses' station. She told him to dress like a doctor himself—khaki pants, light blue shirt, wrinkled tweed jacket—and take the elevator up to the second floor. "From where it stops, you'll have a good view of the nurses' station. Wait until you can pass by it unnoticed."

"What if they see me?"

"They won't pay any attention to you if you keep walking like you're supposed to be here. If they stop you, you could tell them you're a consulting physician from Albuquerque. Do you have a valise?"

"A valise?"

"Something to carry the clothes in."

"Oh, the clothes. Yes, I have something."

"Well, try to make it official-looking. Like a briefcase. You might carry a couple of manila folders too."

"Manila folders?"

"You know, like they use for patient records."

"Oh, of course."

"And, Frank, hurry."

* * *

Blanche kept the TV on while waiting for Frank. The night nurse assigned to her, a large, pleasant woman, stopped in to check on her about eleven-fifteen.

"Aren't you tired, Mrs. Harriman? After what you've been through this evening?"

"I'm just watching the end of this program." It was an old re-run of "Law and Order". "It's relaxing—helps me sleep."

The nurse stood in the room watching the show with her for a few minutes. Blanche groaned inwardly. What if Frank came now? But he didn't. The nurse left.

It was close to midnight by the time he arrived. He quickly ducked into the room, carrying a large brown leather briefcase in his right hand and a couple of manila file folders in his left.

"Hi," Blanche whispered. She thought he looked pretty good. Harris tweed, khakis, just like a doc.

"Hi." He looked around the room to assure himself they were alone before taking out a handkerchief to wipe the beads of perspiration off his forehead.

"Thanks for coming."

"Oh, sure," he said awkwardly.

"You have the clothes?"

"In here." He pointed to the briefcase.

"Well, if you'll excuse me, I'll change in the bathroom." Blanche was swinging her legs over the side of the bed. Frank went to help her.

"Are you sure you're up to this?"

"I'm fine, really," she assured him. "Mitzi's the one who insisted I stay here overnight."

Blanche took the briefcase and headed for the bathroom, trying to keep the hospital gown, which was open in the back, closed around her as she walked. She advised Frank to wait behind the curtain that divided her bed from the empty one near the window so he wouldn't be noticed by anyone walking past.

In a few minutes she came out wearing a pair of over-sized tan pants which she had cinched up high under her breasts with Frank's belt. She put a red polo shirt on top,

and over that, Frank's white tennis sweater with navy trim at the V-neckline. It was long and loose, ample for covering her midsection. On her feet were a pair of buff-colored deck shoes, about three inches too long. Frank tried unsuccessfully to smother a guffaw.

"Sssh."

"Your hair—I brought a hat to cover it." He was grinning as he reached in his pocket for a folded, slightly dirty, white baseball cap. Blanche popped it on her head. Frank guffawed again.

"Ssssh," Blanche hissed. "They'll hear you." She carefully placed the cap over her bandaged scalp and shoved her curls up under it as best she could. Then she went to the bed to stuff a pillow and a blanket under the top sheet, arranging them so they looked like a sleeping body. She switched off the television set, casting the room into almost total darkness.

Frank acted as scout, keeping a watch on the nurses' station through the cracked door of Blanche's room. Two nurses were writing and talking; periodically one of them would leave to check on a patient. Around one o'clock, the nurse with blond hair and glasses was away from the station. Then the other one, the heavy-set nurse who'd stopped in Blanche's room earlier, got up and left too. She went down the south hall, in the direction of the elevators.

"Now," Frank said, motioning for Blanche to come. They stepped out into the corridor and walked swiftly towards the nurses' station. There was no one around. Frank kept a firm hold on Blanche's arm, guiding her past the station toward a stairwell with a red-lighted exit sign. He'd taken note of that when he came in. "Less of a risk than the elevator," he said.

Blanche's head started pounding as they hurried along to the exit. "Wait, I need to stop," she said when they got inside. She closed her eyes and inhaled deeply as she'd learned in yoga classes, and then expelled the air slowly. It was calming, although it didn't do much for the headache.

"Almost home," Frank said, putting a strong hand on her arm, urging her to keep moving down the stairs.

They still had to cross the main lobby. There was a back exit from the hospital, but neither of them knew exactly how to get to it and figured they'd be noticed if they started wandering around trying to find it.

A young man with heavy-rimmed glasses attended the main reception desk, and half a dozen people sat scattered around the large lobby, waiting, reading, dozing. Hardly anyone looked up as Frank and Blanche walked through.

"Good evening," Frank said with a somber nod to the desk man as he steered Blanche toward the door. She kept her head down and leaned heavily on him as though she were infirm. In reality, her hesitant step had more to do with the shoes she was wearing.

A uniformed guard held open the main door while they passed through. He looked at Blanche curiously, but said nothing.

Frank steered her across the parking lot to his car. She had to raise her feet completely off the cracked, uneven pavement with each step in order to keep from tripping in the oversized shoes. It gave her an odd, vaudevillian gait. Frank kept murmuring encouragement. "Just a few more feet."

And then Blanche was safely in the car and Frank was starting up the engine. Her head was pounding, but she

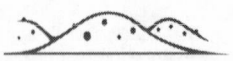

felt relieved. They had made it! Frank wasted no time clearing the parking lot.

"Where to, Madam?" He was trying to be funny.

Where to? She hadn't thought that through yet. She looked at him uncertainly.

"We could go to my place," he suggested.

"Well. . ."

"I doubt if anyone would see us if we took the elevator up from the parking garage."

"Well. . ." She was hesitant. She'd been so focused on getting out of the hospital that she hadn't planned the rest of it. The idea of going back to La Mesa in the middle of the night didn't seem like a good one.

"A motel somewhere out on Cerrillos Road?" Frank suggested.

"A motel?"

"Yeah, a motel. I could stay with you if you'd feel more comfortable, or I could just tuck you in for the night and come back in the morning."

Blanche was thinking. The hospital would find out shortly that she was gone and they'd call La Mesa, then Mitzi, then who knows—the police?

"I'd better go to Mitzi's," she said with sudden decision.

"Mitzi's?"

"Yes, my daughter. She's staying at the El Dorado. She's going to find out about this anyway, so I may as well be the one to tell her."

* * *

Mitzi was literally speechless. Her mouth opened and shut two times while she looked from Blanche to Frank and

back to Blanche. Even then, the only word that came out was "What?" She was clutching the front of the terry-cloth hotel robe she'd hurriedly put on to answer the door.

Frank stood in the hall. "I think I'd better bow out now," he said. "I'll leave the two of you to talk this over. Considering the condition of the patient though, I'd advise her to get a few hours' sleep before delving into all the nitty-gritty details."

"Thanks, Frank," Blanche said, squeezing his hand. "I really appreciate this."

"Just put it on the tab," Frank said.

Blanche managed to smile. Her head was splitting.

"And get some rest. I'll call you in the morning."

"Thanks."

Frank turned away, but he'd only gone two feet when Blanche remembered Juanita. She'd promised to take her to Ortiz' law office in the morning.

"Frank, wait. I need to ask you one more thing. I've got to take Juanita Gomez to Estevan Ortiz' office by nine o'clock, and now I don't have the car."

"Juanita Gomez?"

"Yes, she cleans for me. She used to work for Margaret too. Now she's staying at Ruby Goldmark's. She's got. . .well, she's got a little problem with her papers. We have an appointment to straighten it out. It's very important."

"This really will cost you, you know." Frank smiled. "And I assume there will be a long, detailed explanation of everything over that gourmet dinner you're going to fix for me."

"There will be," she assured him.

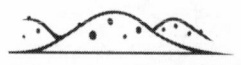

CHAPTER TWENTY

"Are you trying to tell me this will be a boring meeting? As boring as last night, for example?" Mitzi was sitting on the edge of the bed pulling nylon stockings over her slim legs. She sounded peevish.

"Oh Mitzi, please. I told you why I couldn't stay there last night."

"Yes, someone was after you." The sarcasm dripped from her tongue.

Blanche had told Mitzi that someone—someone with a grudge against her—had rigged her car to make the brakes fail. That was why she'd had to leave the hospital in the middle of the night. Whoever it was might try to track her down in the hospital where she would be defenseless.

"And then what?" Mitzi had demanded.

"It's perfectly obvious," Blanche had said. "Whoever it was would find me and finish off the job."

"Mother, really. You've been reading too many novels. You're getting carried away."

Blanche had flung herself flat down onto the bed at that point, and thrown her arm across her eyes. "We can talk about it in the morning," she said. "I've got to get some sleep." She pretended to fall into a coma-like sleep and kept her eyes tightly closed even while she sensed Mitzi peering at her. Eventually she heard her telephone the hospital to say that Blanche was safe. "She's very upset about the accident," Mitzi explained in hushed tones. "She's spending the night with me." Pause. "Yes, I understand; I accept full responsibility."

Now, after a restless night that left them both feeling edgy, they were getting dressed to meet Juanita and Frank downstairs. Blanche had tried to dissuade Mitzi from coming along, but it was a lost battle.

"I'm not letting you go off on your own," Mitzi said firmly as she stepped into a pair of tan pumps and picked an invisible bit of dust off her linen dress. "I came to Santa Fe expecting to cheer you up over the loss of Margaret and instead I see you caught up in some cloak and dagger drama."

"I told you, this is all very complicated," Blanche said. She was buttoning the pink shift Mitiz had lent her. It was cut loose enough to fit. Shoes were a problem though, and Blanche had to settle for a pair of Mitzi's flat sandals, open at the back.

"Complicated is an understatement," Mitzi said. "And I don't get what Juanita has to do with it."

Blanche was being busy with her hair.

"I don't know how you got yourself into this mess," Mitzi persisted.

"We'd better get going," Blanche said. "I told Frank we'd meet him in the lobby at ten to nine."

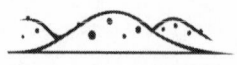

"Tell me more about this Frank," Mitzi said while they were riding down in the elevator.

"He's a good friend."

"I can see that."

Blanche laughed.

"Does *he* believe someone's after you?"

Mitzi's question went unanswered because the elevator door opened at that moment and they found Frank and Juanita waiting in the El Dorado lobby.

As Frank drove them towards Ortiz' law office on Marcy St., Blanche patted Juanita's arm reassuringly. Poor thing was as tight as a wind-up toy. She looked over the form Juanita had filled out for the Immigration and Naturalization Service and found herself staring, fixated, at the neat, schoolgirl handwriting, oblivious to the words themselves. She'd seen that handwriting before.

* * *

The session with Ortiz took two hours and fifteen minutes. He carefully went over the steps that lay ahead for Juanita, explaining each one in his elegant Spanish, occasionally translating a phrase to make certain that Blanche understood it too. He told Juanita she'd have to return to Mexico within five days. Later, perhaps in six to eight weeks, with Blanche agreeing to act as her "host", she could re-enter the U.S. and bring her son, Benito, for eye surgery at the University of New Mexico Medical Center. Ortiz would contact Juanita in Mexico as soon as the necessary paperwork cleared U.S. Immigration.

Federal charges would be filed against Nita, Juanita's cousin, for the illegal transfer of her social security num-

ber to Juanita, and there would be fines levied against them both. It could end up costing Juanita everything she had earned in the past year, Ortiz said.

The money was a minor point now. Ortiz had filed another set of papers to ensure Juanita would get her inheritance no matter what happened. But it could take six months, possibly a year, before it was in her hands.

He'd also talked with a sympathetic Immigration officer, a man who'd been born in Mexico and understood the desperation that drove Juanita to work in the U.S. illegally. He arranged for her to meet with this officer in Albuquerque before she boarded the bus back to Chihuahua, so she'd have a personal advocate in the agency.

Juanita was still pale as they came out to the lobby, but some of the tension had left her face. She no longer had to shoulder this whole burden by herself. She owed much to *Senora Harriman* for helping her.

* * *

"Your brake line was cut, probably with a hacksaw or file," Dick Masters told Blanche. She'd excused herself to make the call outside The Shed Restaurant where, although it was not quite noon, the lunch line extended out into the patio. "It's not the type of thing that happens by itself."

"You mean someone had to do it deliberately."

"Right. And once the line is cut, the brake fluid drains out. Oh, it might leave enough in there for a few stops, but then it brings down all the fluid from the master cylinder and—whammo—no brakes."

"That's what happened. I was coming down the hill and

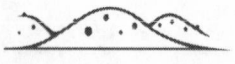

suddenly there was no brake-power. I tried the emergency brake, but it didn't work either."

"That's cable-operated, separate from the regular brakes. It only affects the rear wheels. It slows you a little, but if you're going downhill like you were, it doesn't do anything to stop you."

"You're sure about all this?"

"Positive. This was a deliberate cut. I think you better call the police."

Blanche thanked Masters and hung up. She'd left Frank, Mitzi and Juanita sitting inside at the table, telling them to order the blue corn enchiladas for her. She had to make a couple of calls and would be there in a minute. She dialed another number on her emergency cell phone.

"K.G. Labs," the receptionist answered.

"This is Dr. Harriman," Blanche said in a clipped, businesslike voice. "I'm calling to learn the results of a drug sample I sent over earlier this week."

"Dr. Harriman, we've been trying to reach you." The receptionist's voice went up two notches.

"Oh?"

"Let me connect you with Mr. Gabaldon."

"Mr. Gabaldon?"

"Kenneth Gabaldon, our director. Just a moment please."

Blanche felt a twinge of anticipation as she was put on hold for Gabaldon.

"Dr. Harriman, the medication you brought us—did you prescribe it for Mrs. Forbes?"

"*Miss* Forbes," Blanche corrected. She was trying to think fast. Gabaldon must know she hadn't prescribed

the pills. Dr. Hillman's name was right there on the bottle. Why was he asking?

"*Miss* Forbes," Gabaldon repeated. "Did you prescribe the Omeprazole for her?"

"No," she said.

"How did you obtain it?"

"I took it."

"You *took* it?"

"For analysis."

"I see," Gabaldon said. There was an awkward pause.

"Is there something wrong?"

"We need another day to be sure," Gabaldon said, his voice businesslike. "We still have another test to complete."

"It's been three days, Mr. Gabaldon. You promised results in forty-eight hours."

"Well, it's a little more complicated."

"Complicated? What do you mean?"

"Our tests aren't final yet, so I can't draw any definite conclusions."

"What's going on?" Blanche's voice rose, causing several heads to turn in her direction.

"The Omeprazole may be tainted," Gabaldon said.

"Tainted with what?"

"This could be quite serious, Dr. Harriman," Gabaldon said instead of answering her question directly. "You may be asked for additional information as to how you obtained these samples."

"What?"

"I'm sorry, Dr. Harriman, but there's really not any more I can tell you right now. I suggest you keep yourself available in the event we need to reach you later on today or in the morning." Gabaldon hung up.

* * *

"Mother, what's wrong?" Mitzi's garlic-buttered French bread stopped halfway to her mouth.

Blanche was glad to be sitting down. She believed her knees were starting to buckle.

"Oh nothing unexpected, really." She tried to sound calm as she told them what Dick Masters had said about her brakes.

"Exactly what you suspected," Frank said somberly, patting her hand.

Mitzi, for once, was rendered speechless and she looked like her eyes were about to pop out of their sockets.

"He feels I ought to report it to the police, which I shall do after lunch."

"By all means," Frank said. "But first, you'd better concentrate on these enchiladas first. You look like you could use a little fuel."

"Mother, what is going on!" Mitzi demanded.

"I think I'm beginning to understand it," Blanche said. She dipped a piece of crusty garlic bread into the thick red chili sauce. "You see, I found a very curious list of names in Margaret's library book a few days after she died." She could sense Juanita's body stiffening. "I think maybe you know something about it," she said, looking meaningfully towards her.

"*Si, señora.*" Juanita kept her face down and stared at the plate which she had barely touched.

"Why don't you and I have a talk about it after lunch?"

* * *

Frank drove them back to La Mesa. They decided it would be best for Juanita to take the parking garage elevator up to Ruby's apartment. Blanche insisted that she and Mitzi be dropped off at the front entrance, however. She gave a hearty greeting to J.J. Chavez as they came in.

"Mrs. Harriman, it's good to see you," he said. "I'm sorry about the accident. Hope everything's all right."

"Thanks, J.J. It's good to be back."

When they got to her apartment, she went straight to the telephone and dialed the Santa Fe Police Department. She asked for Lieutenant Otero.

"I have some interesting new information for you" she said, reminding him she'd been in to see him a few days ago.

"Yes, Ma'am, I'm listening," he said.

She reported how she'd narrowly averted getting herself killed, and what Dick Masters had told her about the brake line. "And I find it very curious that Dr. Hillman died in a similar accident just last night," she said.

"He was coming down Dead Man's curve," Otero said. "I've just read the report."

"I wouldn't be surprised if his brake line was cut too."

"We'll check it out." Otero's tone was official.

"Dick Masters told me that even if a car has crashed and burned, you could still determine whether the brake line had been cut."

Otero thanked her for her call and told her to take it easy.

"Come on," she said, turning to Mitzi when she hung up. She knew Mitzi had been listening intently to her side of the conversation. "We're going upstairs to Ruby's. I need to have a talk with Juanita."

CHAPTER TWENTY-ONE

Under Blanche's very direct questioning, Juanita admitted she'd used the master key from Housekeeping to get into the business office at night. Miss Forbes had asked her to look in the big file cabinet for a folder called Life-Care Annuity Program. She had written down the words for her. Miss Forbes told her to copy down the names of the people listed in the folder.

"She said I should not let anyone see me," Juanita said nervously as she told Blanche about the favor she had done for Miss Forbes. "She said it was very important."

"Do you know what these little notes mean?" Blanche pointed to the pencilled-in words—*here, none, away*—next to each name.

Juanita shook her head.

"You can trust me, Juanita. I think you know that now."

"*Sí Señora.*"

"I think the reason Miss Forbes died so suddenly was connected to something she knew about the people on

this list. Did Miss Forbes say anything to you about these people?

"She said. .. " Juanita hesitated.

"It's very important, Juanita."

"She said she was worried about them."

"Why was she worried?"

"She said they were dying too fast."

"I think someone may have killed Miss Forbes because she was trying to help these people," Blanche said, carefully watching Juanita's reaction.

"*Dios Mio!*" Juanita made the sign of the cross quickly across her forehead.

"That's why you must tell me anything that you think might be important."

"I just wrote their names as Miss Forbes told me to," said Juanita, obviously frightened. Her eyes met Blanche's for a second, then flicked away.

"What else?" Blanche prompted.

"I heard you talking on the *teléfono* about Miss Forbes' pills," she said uncertainly.

"You mean the new pills, the Omeprazole? What about them?"

"Dr. Hillman delivered them."

"Dr. Hillman?"

"*Sí*, Dr. Hillman."

"Are you sure?"

Juanita seemed to be gaining courage and looked up to meet Blanche's eyes. "I was there. I answered the door and he handed me the little package."

"Did he ever deliver pills before?"

"No, I don't think so. The delivery man from *la farmacia*

always leaves them downstairs for Miss Forbes or myself to pick up."

"Did you tell Miss Forbes?"

"No." Juanita looked frightened.

"And what did you do with them?"

"I put them in the cabinet in the bathroom."

CHAPTER TWENTY-TWO

Blanche thought it was a long shot, but worth a try. Lucy Begay, a registered nurse, had spent most of her professional life running chronic disease screening clinics on the Navajo Reservation. She was retired and living in Albuquerque now. Blanche had met her a couple of times through Margaret.

"What are the names?" Lucy asked when Blanche telephoned to ask for her help.

"One is Anthony Grace, the administrator up here at La Mesa. The other one was the attending physician, Avery Hillman. Unfortunately, he died last night in an automobile accident."

"Hillman? Kind of a nice-looking guy? I remember him," Lucy said. "He worked out of the Window Rock office. What happened?"

"His car went off the road coming down from Los Alamos after a meeting of the State Medical Society. Supposedly an accident, but I'm not so sure."

"Oh yeah?"

"It's a long story—I'll fill you in later. What I'd like to know, is whether Grace and Hillman were connected in the past. They both worked for the Navajo Health Authority some years back."

"You know, I think Hillman got into some trouble at Window Rock," Lucy remembered. "He was accused of double dipping and the Navajo Health Authority fired him. It was a real mess."

"Double dipping?"

"Yeah, he'd made up some bogus consulting firm, which was really himself, and billed the federal government for consulting fees. All while he was on the N.H.A. payroll. He and some young guy were in on it."

"Did he face charges?'

"I'm not sure. He left N.H.A. in a hurry. I don't know what happened to him after that."

"Was the young guy by any chance Anthony Grace?"

"That name doesn't ring a bell," Lucy said. "It was some hotshot from the East Coast. But I. . . gee, that doesn't sound like the name."

"Could you check it out?"

"I've still got some friends over at Window Rock. I'll ask them to pull Hillman's records."

"Do you think you can get back to me before five o'clock?" Blanche looked at her watch. It was quarter to four.

"Whoa, that gives me a whole hour before they close," Lucy said. "You mind telling me what this is all about?"

"I will, as soon as you call back."

"Have you got a subpoena for this, lady?"

Blanche laughed.

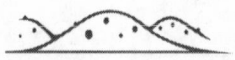

"Please, Lucy, it's important."

"I'll see what I can do," Lucy said.

* * *

Blanche was steeped in fragile bubbles, listening to them pop all around her, and thinking hard. The information Lucy Begay called back with reinforced the urgency of the situation. Tomorrow would be too late. If something were going to happen, it was likely to be tonight. And if she were smart, she'd be prepared.

She got out of the steaming bath, wrapped a towel around herself, and headed to the phone in the bedroom. Mitzi, who was sticking to her like glue, was watching the five-thirty news in the living room.

"Ruby? Listen, I need your help tonight." She cupped her hand over the receiver so the sound of her voice wouldn't carry.

"Sorry, honey, I've got other plans tonight," Ruby said. She was going to be difficult.

"Ruby, I swear, I won't ask you to do another thing."

"OK, so what is it?" Ruby said, resigned.

Blanche explained the plan.

"Be here by quarter to eleven," she instructed. "Leave your beads on the door just as you do every night. Don't let anyone see you."

"Become invisible?"

"Exactly. I was thinking you could take the west elevator down to the parking garage, and then take the east elevator back up to the first floor. That way you wouldn't have to cross the main lobby."

"Are you sure you're not working for the C.I.A.?"

"I need to talk to Esther too."

"I'll do it if Esther will," Ruby finally said.

"Thanks, Ruby. I really appreciate this."

Esther was more enthusiastic than Blanche expected.

"Should I bring my bat?" she asked. "I have one, for when my grandson visits."

"By all means. And a loud whistle if you've got one."

"What about Frank? Are you asking him to help?"

"I don't think so," Blanche said. "He wouldn't go along with this. He's too much of a worrywart."

"We could use Helen," Esther said. "She carries one of those battery-operated emergency alarms with her all the time. It could come in handy."

"Good idea. I'll call her."

Blanche expected that Helen would be hesitant about getting involved, and she was right. But she didn't give her much of a chance to articulate her objections.

"We need you," she told her. "Your wheelchair can fit right inside the bathroom. We'd all feel a lot better having you with us to call the police in case things got out of control."

"Well. . .all right. . .I'll try," Helen promised a little uncertainly.

"We're counting on you, Helen."

Blanche hung up the telephone and turned around to find Mitzi staring at her. In her enthusiasm for the plan, she'd forgotten to keep her voice down.

The moment of truth had come.

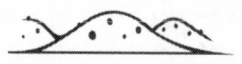

* * *

Blanche didn't know how much she could actually eat because her stomach was twitching like a Mexican jumping bean. But Mitzi had agreed to appear with her in the dining room and help her play up the effects of her recent accident.

"You don't look too bad, considering," Bud Rosenblum said gallantly when he saw her with the white bandage tied dramatically across her forehead. ("I want to look wounded, not pathetic," Blanche had instructed Mitzi as she arranged it.)

"My daughter's come to help me out for a few days," Blanche said, introducing them.

"You take care of this lady for us," Bud said to Mitzi. "We don't want to lose her."

Mitzi smiled rather stiffly and assured him she'd do her best.

Blanche waved to Lenore Richards, and to Reggie Salazar, and to anyone else she recognized. She could feel the curious stares of everyone around her. No doubt, word had gotten around about her accident and probably about her midnight escape from the hospital too. There weren't many secrets at La Mesa.

Ah, there was Christine Wilson coming in now. Mitzi had telephoned her office and asked if she could get some sleeping pills for Blanche.

"Tell her it's been such an upsetting twenty-four hours that I'm a nervous wreck," Blanche had instructed.

Christine had been obliging. She said she'd call in for a doctor's approval and bring the pills down to the dining room.

"We sure would appreciate it," Mitzi had said. "Mother has to get some sleep or she'll never recover from all this."

"Halcion," Christine said, handing Mitzi a small brown bottle. "Give her one at bedtime."

Christine's eyes were puffy and dark underneath. She'd probably gotten a call during the night telling her about the accident, Blanche thought.

"I'm so sorry about Dr. Hillman," Blanche said. "How's Mr. Grace taking it?"

"Shocked, of course. He's still in the office, going through the necessary paperwork."

Blanche nodded sympathetically..

They asked Christine to join them for lunch, but she said she had some work to finish. She promised to check on Blanche in the morning. "You just give her one of these," she instructed Mitzi, tapping the little pill bottle, "and she'll be out like a baby tonight."

"Thanks very much. We really appreciate it." Mitzi popped the bottle into her purse. Neither she nor Blanche had the slightest intention of Blanche swallowing a sleeping pill; they were just using Christine to help set the trap.

After dinner, Blanche made a show of waiting in the lobby with Mitzi until the yellow cab arrived to take her back to the El Dorado Hotel.

"I don't feel right about leaving," Mitzi whispered to Blanche.

"You have to. It's the only way it'll work."

"I'll never forgive myself if something happens," she said.

Then, as they spotted the cab coming up the drive, Mitzi delivered her line, loud enough for J.J. Chavez and the

receptionist, and anyone else within earshot to overhear, "Take your sleeping pill now, and I'll see you in the morning."

* * *

Blanche turned off the light on the bedside table and began the long wait. She heard sounds she'd never paid attention to before. The elevator down the hall, a scraping of a chair in the next apartment, the muffled noise from a television set nearby. Around twelve-thirty, she might have dozed for a few minutes but she came to, alert, as soon as her leg touched one of the ice packs she'd stuck under the sheet for just that reason, to jog her back if she started to slip off.

She wondered what Arthur would have thought about her plan. Maybe she *should* have enlisted Frank's support. She thought about Mitzi and how courageous it was of her really, to go back to the hotel and wait. Just so she didn't get too nervous and blow it by coming back early!

She thought about her grandchildren, Kristen and Jeff, whom she hadn't seen since Christmas. She should spend more time with them, take them somewhere.

England? Italy? Her mind danced across Europe. France would be nice. Or maybe Scandinavia—she had a friend they could visit in Stockholm and then they could go on to Denmark. She glanced at the clock. It was almost quarter of two. She was getting sleepy again, and forced herself to daydream about bicycling around Denmark with Kristen and Jeff. They'd travel with backpacks. She thought about what she would take, and she wondered how she could get it all into a backpack?

A shuffling sound came from the bathroom, then silence. Blanche was instantly alert. She looked around the room, her eyes adjusted to the near darkness, and picked out the familiar shapes of her chair, her dressing table, her bureau. She listened intently, but there was nothing else. It was deadly quiet again.

Her sixth sense told her the time was close. She strained, trying to pick up the tiniest of sounds. Nothing from the closet, nothing from the bathroom now. She felt alone, on her own.

And suddenly she heard it. It was the clicking sound of the front door opening.

Then nothing.

She listened. One, maybe two minutes passed. She saw a momentary flash of light from the direction of the living room, and then it was black again.

She waited, perfectly still, straining so hard to listen that she stopped breathing. Her eyes were open, watching for the first movement. She thought she smelled the faint scent of Old Spice, but it might have been her imagination.

Then, before she had time to react, a bright beam of light blinded her and a gloved hand came down over her mouth. She was instantly paralyzed, the whistle clutched uselessly in her clenched fist.

"Perhaps you've been expecting me?" Anthony Grace said with a contemptuous smile curling his lips. In his other hand was a long thin hypodermic needle. He was aiming it directly for the soft flesh of her upper arm.

Blanche's eyes bulged with terror as she wriggled her body to the side, trying desperately to avoid the needle. With her mouth covered, she could emit only a muffled groaning from deep in her throat.

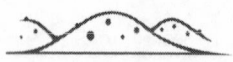

Suddenly all hell broke loose.

Helen sounded her emergency alarm from the bathroom.

"A-yee!" Esther—of all people—shrieked as she charged out of the closet with her baseball bat and whacked Grace over the back, toppling him down sideways across Blanche's body in the bed.

"Arrrgh." Grace reeled off the bed, dropping to the floor on his hands and knees.

"The head, go for his head," Ruby shouted, driving a broom into him ruthlessly.

He grabbed at Ruby's legs and knocked her over. The lamp on the dresser came crashing down. Ruby lay still.

The bathroom door slammed shut. Helen had locked herself in and was no doubt calling the police.

Blanche recovered her wits. She hurled an ice bag across the room, causing Grace to reel for a second as he went for Esther.

He charged Esther and managed to disarm her, grabbing the fat end of the bat. Then he swirled around and aimed it at Blanche like a bayonet.

Blanche saw it coming and in a split second rolled herself off the bed, trapping herself between it and the wall. There was nowhere else to go. She couldn't fit underneath the bed.

But Esther was bashing Grace from behind, this time with a long metal pipe, which Blanche recognized as an attachment from her vacuum cleaner. Grace whirled around to defend himself and for a few seconds he and Esther dueled, he with the bat, she with the vacuum attachment.

"Murderer!" she screamed. Her hair had come loose from its perfect French knot and streamed wildly around her face.

Blanche was on her knees, crawling out from the side of the bed and reaching for the broom that still lay on the floor next to Ruby who was now moaning softly. She was going to try and ram Grace from the rear.

"FREEZE." The overhead light went on as a man's voice boomed out the command. Lieutenant Otero stood there, a gun pointed in the direction of Grace. Behind him, standing white-faced in the doorway, was Mitzi.

CHAPTER TWENTY-THREE

Three days later, Lieutenant Otero sat in Blanche's living room at La Mesa trying to fill in the missing pieces.

"When I found that list of names, I knew Margaret was on to something," Blanche explained. "It turned out they were all signed up for La Mesa's Life-Care Program and they were dying off at a pretty fast rate."

"Sort of a hit list, huh?" Otero, who was taking an official statement from her, held the list of names in his hand.

"Right. The people who had family members visiting them regularly were fairly safe. They're the ones marked `here' on the list." Blanche pointed to Margaret's notations. "But if there were no family members around to monitor conditions on a regular basis, she wrote `none' or `away.' They were the vulnerable ones. It would be easy for Dr. Hillman to overdose them with something lethal and no one would ever know the difference. I think that's exactly what happened to Leland Strel and Peggy Masterson."

"This is your own theory?" Otero looked sharply at Blanche.

"It is."

"Very interesting." Otero picked up the cup of lemongrass tea Blanche had served him and raised it to his nose to sniff. He set it back down in the saucer.

"The world doesn't tend to question it much when someone over seventy-five or eighty dies," Blanche said. "It's almost expected that you could die at any moment once you get to that age."

"What put you on to the pills?"

"It was a piece of luck, in a way. I had the suspicion that Hillman had prescribed the wrong pills and was trying to cover it up by lying about Margaret having a bad heart. You see, I *knew* there was nothing wrong with her heart!"

"That's why you took them to K.G. Labs?"

"Yes. I wasn't thinking about anything as dramatic as cyanide. But I did get more suspicious when Juanita told me that Dr. Hillman personally delivered the pills to Margaret's apartment."

Otero told her that K.G. Labs had called the police after finding minute traces of granular cyanide dusting several of the Omeprazole capsules. They'd run the cyanide test after a scent-sensitive technician that K.G. Labs called "The Nose" had detected a suspicious odor on the pills, an odor not associated with Omeprazole. A Prussian Blue test indicated the presence of cyanide.

"This guy figured one of the capsules must have been emptied of the Omeprazole and re-filled with cyanide," Otero said. "When the bottle got jostled around, some cyanide residue probably leaked out onto the other capsules."

Blanche nodded. Now she understood why K.G. Labs had tried to stall her. They thought she had something to

do with the tainted pills, especially after they found out she wasn't a physician.

"The Medical Investigator's Office issued a permit to exhume Miss Forbes' body immediately. They've confirmed that she died of cyanide poisoning," Otero said.

"Now it all fits together," Blanche said. "Margaret must have had a pretty clear idea of what was happening to these annuity holders. When Grace and Hillman learned she was on to them, they decided to get rid of her. It didn't matter exactly which day Margaret took the lethal pill; sooner or later she was going to get it. Hillman would be the doctor on call and could explain away any abnormalities in the appearance of the body. I'm sure he calculated that with the one cyanide pill gone from the bottle, there'd never be any evidence to link him to the murder."

"Clever," Otero said, shaking his head. "But what was in it for Grace and Hillman? They couldn't keep the millions of dollars they made on these annuities. It all belonged to La Mesa."

"It wasn't about money," Blanche said. "I believe it was Grace's ambition. I know from talking with Christine Wilson that he was aiming for a corporate position at Esteem Enterprises. La Mesa del Sol was being used as a stepping stone. He had to prove that he could run a really successful operation, one that made a big profit."

"What about Hillman? What was in it for him?"

"That's more complicated. They go back a long way."

"Does this have to do with the snake design in the rug?" The night Grace was arrested, Blanche had started rambling to Otero about the caduceus design in a Navajo rug she'd seen in Dr. Hillman's office.

"That's what linked them," she said. "When I saw the rug had the initials N.H.A. woven into it, I figured he must have worked for the Navajo Health Authority. I knew that Grace had worked there too. It seemed likely that they'd known each other before coming here."

Otero still looked puzzled.

"I called a friend of mine who worked as a nurse on the Reservation for many years. She had some contacts at the N.H.A. office in Window Rock, and she checked them out."

"Checked them out." Otero said it flat, like a statement.

"She remembered that Hillman had been involved in some double dipping years ago, charging the federal government twice for the same work." Blanche allowed a slight professorial tone to come into her voice as she explained the facts to Otero. "He lost his credentials and his reputation for a while. Anthony Grace, then known as Tony Gracey, was involved too, but nothing happened to him."

"You mean Hillman took the rap?"

"Right. Gracey got off free."

"Then years later, Gracey—or Grace—offers Hillman the house doctor job at La Mesa as a sort of belated thank-you," Otero speculated, trying to put the pieces together.

"That's the way I figure it," Blanche agreed.

"But how did Grace talk him into the murder scheme?"

"We'll never know for sure," Blanche said. "Hillman was a loner, never married, not close to anyone here. I think he was a weak man who became a tool of Grace's driving ambition. I suspect Grace pressured him. Maybe he promised him a cushy position with Esteem Enterprises if he cooperated."

"Then when Hillman got rattled and threatened to tell all, Grace shut him up permanently?" Otero *had* followed through with Blanche's suggestion to check the burned rubble of Dr. Hillman's car to see if the brake line had been cut. It had.

"Right, the same way he tried to stop me."

"He's been booked on charges of murder and attempted murder in connection with Hillman's death and the attempt on your life. Additional charges are pending. In the meantime, they're holding him in the Santa Fe County Jail."

"Quite a comedown for an ambitious young man."

"He may prefer jail to another evening with you and your troops."

Blanche laughed.

"You know," Otero said with uncharacteristic humility, "I didn't think you had your marbles lined up straight."

Blanche wrinkled her brow and then deciphered what he was trying to say. "Thank you, Lieutenant. I think that's a compliment."

"You took a big risk though," Otero said. "You should have called me."

"You never would have let me do it," Blanche said. "And Anthony Grace may never have been caught."

"You're lucky your daughter was here. She had the sense to let me know what was going on."

"I'm indebted to you," Blanche said. "You arrived in the nick of time."

And Mitzi showed some proper steel, she thought. She'd even called Frank Zanders that night and had him guarding the hallway outside Blanche's apartment in case something went wrong and Grace tried to escape.

Blanche smiled to herself, trying to picture how Frank would have tried to tackle Grace. In reality, Frank was so frightened that he could barely speak when it was all over.

* * *

After Lieutenant Otero left, Blanche went into the kitchen to get two "gourmet" *coq au vin* dinners out of the freezer and put together a romaine and radicchio salad which she would serve with her original lemon and poppyseed dressing. She also arranged a fancy assortment of chocolate eclairs, chocolate petits fours, and chocolate truffles on a silver dessert tray. Frank was partial to chocolate.

While dinner was cooking, well, while it was thawing, she planned to have a long, lovely bubble bath and concentrate on something perfectly divine to wear. Frank liked her in green. . . But then, black was so seductive. . .

THE END

CPSIA information can be obtained
at www.ICGtesting.com
Printed in the USA
FSOW01n0112300817
38018FS